<u>Acknowledgements</u>

God, who created me.

Jesus, who saved me.

Mom, who raised me.

Dad, who awakened me.

Sister, who taught me.

Wife, who loves me.

Son, who energizes me.

Editor, who pushed me.

Reader, who enjoyed a story by me, fingers crossed.

Day Nine

It had been 168 hours, 10,080 minutes, and 604,800 seconds since my dad had passed, not that time mattered much after that moment. In fact, the only time concern amongst the family was the amount of time a dead man had before he needed to be buried. Superstition 101 said no more than ten days, and today was day nine. It is funny how death can influence the most Stallworth Christians to trust in the mysteries of old wives' tales- no questions asked. Maybe years ago, ten days was the customary length of time. Who knows? But ten days was agreed upon, and there had been a countdown ever since. The past eight days had been exactly the same: sleep, wake up, daydream, sleep, eat, daydream, sleep, repeat. I purposely never tried to come out of that cloudy feeling of sleepiness. Every moment that I was able to escape to the REM world, a world where I could change, philosophize, accept, and awake into a daydream just to start the process over was a gift that being awake only stripped from me. I was perfectly fine not being consciously present and not acknowledging that tomorrow was my Dad's funeral. Until day nine, I was able to get up as I pleased, not talk to people as I pleased, not answer my phone as I pleased, and not eat food as I pleased. Today that all was supposed to cease. Today was preparation day. Unfortunately, for me, the reality of my dad's funeral started on that evening of day nine... I could not go to bed. My body had had enough of the intentional sleepwalking, and purpose was back in the mix of my decisions. I had to be purposeful because purpose is the fruit of reason. I needed to make sure I went to bed at a good time, so I could wake up and take care of funeral preparations. I had been staying under the fog of grogginess to prevent me from thinking about the reality of my father passing. Purposely forcing myself to get in bed, I came out that fog as I had to acknowledge the reason, I was doing it. I tossed and turned all night until finally, I gave up on sleeping. I got up and starting my day during the wee hours of the morning. I took the suit I intended to wear out of the garment bag and inspected it. Over the years, I had collected eight suits of various blacks, blues, and grays. Those were always the suggested colors of suits given to me from my dad. I used the word collected because I never wore them. It was almost comical. I would try them on, buy them, alter them, then hang them up in my closet, each in its designated space only to be worn for whatever special occasion had come up that required a suit in the first place- mostly funerals or weddings. I heard it said once that there is no difference. Anyway, I laid everything out right down to the accessories-socks, shoes, everything. I could not believe tomorrow I would be in the mirror buttoning up my shirt, tying my tie, and making sure my shoes shined, all for moment I would bury my father. The man, who had taught me about the suit game. The man who had taught me how to do what I thought as a child was "mission impossible," to button the small buttons on each one of my sleeves with the opposite hand. I was now doing all this for him. I am sure he never thought that what he was teaching me would someday be used at his own funeral. It worked out that I had gotten up earlier than necessary. I got to take my time and not be rushed, like the sunrise was doing. Nobody else was up yet, which was perfect. It was mysteriously quiet, like God had hit the mute button and told the angels, "Quiet on the set," as he attentively listened for my needs. I finished inspecting my suit, ran the iron over a few wrinkles, and hung it up. Next, what to wear today? I needed to hit the barbershop this morning, so comfortability was the move. I figured tomorrow I would be tucked in and tailored all day. So, I went with gray sweatpants, the foundation of any comfortable outfit. You can always build from there however you want. I finished dressing, quietly snuck downstairs to make a bowl of cereal, and went back to my room to eat it. I did not want to chance somebody waking up to talk this early in the morning. That would have been the equivalent of rap music before 10am in the barbershop. First thing on the agenda, I needed to head to the barbershop to get my haircut. I finished my cereal, brushed my teeth, and was successfully out of the house before anybody woke up only to have to return after being roughed up by the temperature. It was a cold warmth, like a whooping from your mother. It is going to sting, but her love for you will not let her keep whooping you too long. I quietly went upstairs to grab a jacket and tip toed back out of the house. I was lucky that the last time I had left the house, when I got back, the driveway was filled with cars. So, I parked on the street. If not for that, I would have been blocked in and waking people up this morning. As I walked to my car, I could see the bridge that led out onto the main road, just outside of the subdivision. My Dad had lived in this house for 21 years, and for 21 years I always said I would walk that bridge and overcome my fear of heights, but I never had. Why not today? Why wait? The passing of my father had me looking at my honorable mention bucket list stuff like "Do everything you want to do when you can because you may not have that time again. Especially positive stuff, you can keep delaying the foolishness." Only in my father's death did the often said but rarely felt, "Time waits for no one," become painstakingly true. See, I always knew my father would pass, but I also always knew when my father would pass, until he actually passed. With all the naivety of an untouched Amazon Tribe in the middle of Times Square, I really thought I controlled the timeline of death. I had a reasonable timeline for my father, and "now" was not on that timeline. As I walked to my car contemplating whether I should drive or walk, I was interrupted with an answer.

Auntie

"Whatcha doing? It looks like you were talking to yourself.

Dang, I was trying to get out of the house without waking anybody up.

Well, I guess you failed. What you about to do?

I was heading to the barbershop. Couldn't decide if I was going to drive or walk.

How about both!

Huh?

Both, give me two seconds to grab a coat and brush my teeth.

Naw, you good Aunite. You don't have to do that.

I know I'm good. That's why I solved your problem. You can drive and walk; now hold your horses. I know you looking for some alone time. You will get that on the way back because I am not going to pick you up. I am making breakfast this morning, and I need to pick up some things from the grocery store before everybody wakes up and the rest of the family makes it over. I will let you drive my car since you know these streets better than me. You can drive us out and point me to the nearest grocery store when you get to the barbershop, plus it will be warmer and more comfortable to walk back. Here! Catch my keys. I will be out in just a minute.

Ok.

Thanks for waiting on me nephew. I could tell you didn't want to.

Naw, auntie its cool. No problem.

Well good because that's just a growing pain of life. Doing stuff, you don't really want to do, because you love the person you are doing it for. Plus, you owe me.

I owe you?

Yes, indeed. I remember when you were little, begging your momma to stay the night over our house because we had a big game room. We had everything any kid could want in there, from video game systems to a basketball arcade. One night you were having so much fun, you asked could you stay over. Your uncle and I didn't mind at all. Your mom kept asking you, "Are you sure," because she knew your dad was not coming back to get you until tomorrow. You nodded yes and ran back up to the game room. I bet it was not an hour, maybe two hours later, you got sleepy. You came downstairs crying and said…

I want my momma.

Exactly, you want your momma, your daddy, you want to go home. All of that! You know me and your uncle do not have any kids. Your uncle was not used to all that whining and had no interest in trying to get used to it while he was in the bed. See, nephew I knew you could not hang, but you were having so much fun in the game room, I decided to give you a shot and let you stay the night. You had those tears just running down your face and looked so sad. I told you to put your shoes on, and I would take you home. Your uncle was mad at me for a couple of days behind that. He said I was spoiling you, making you soft, and your daddy agreed. But I took you home anyway. We got in the car, and your whole attitude changed. It was not a tear in sight. I felt duped. The whole ride home you kept saying look auntie look it's a fingernail. I was so mad thinking your uncle was right about spoiling you, I ignored you the whole way to your house. It was not until I dropped you off and saw how happy you were that I stopped being mad. On the way back home, I looked up to see what you were talking about.

What was it?

You don't remember? You were talking about the moon. It looked like a fingernail. You always had a vivid imagination. That is why you were always getting in trouble for lying all the time.

C'mon auntie.

I am serious but let me shut up and give you what you wanted.

What is that?

Peace and quiet.

This was my first day out the house since I left my dad at the hospital. It was only a couple of miles to the barbershop. Before you interrupted my plans, I was leaning heavily towards walking. My father's death had me thinking about all the bucket list stuff I had been putting off with a different mentality. One of those items on my list was conquering my fear of heights. I thought I could start my first day out from isolated mourning by walking the bridge on my way to the barbershop, scratching that off my bucket list. It would be a

Dedication Walk to my dad because if he were here, I most certainly would not be walking. I guess now it would be a Dedication Walk back to the house.

Well, you can cut the radio on if you want.

Thanks.

Nephew, I know I said I would be quiet, but nephew where is the barbershop? We have been riding long enough for a barbershop to have shown up, especially in this cool air.

It's coming up here on the right.

Okay, just know I was playing. I will come pick you up. This is a nice stroll from the house.

Thank you, but I want to walk.

I feel you. I need to start walking myself, at least that's what your uncle keeps hinting.

Well, I guess that's growing pains, right?

Huh?

Doing stuff, you do not really want to do, because you love the person, you are doing it for.

Ha, boy you lucky we at the barbershop now or you would be walking the rest of the way. Now where is the grocery store?

You know I love you too, auntie. Just keep straight; it will be three lights up. You will see it at that intersection.

Thank ya nephew, and love you, too!

Call me if you get lost.

Will do. Hey nephew, here ya go.

What is this? I don't need no money.

I know, but the barber does, so use this.

Thank you.

Uh huh. Be careful walking back.

Barbershop Antics

BARBERSHOP:

Welcome to Vee's! What up, Trey?

Not too much, Vee. How you?

Busy, early this morning as you can see. What are you doing up here so early? You know Rasheem isn't here yet. Does he know you coming up here?

Yeah, we talked yesterday.

Ok cool. You may want to text him just in case.

Alright.

Yo, who was that that dropped you off? Ha, ha, ha.

You wild, man. That was my aunt.

Barbershop patron: She single, I would be a cool uncle.

Relax, y'all with the foolishness early this morning.

You know how they get? Plus, Jay was in here earlier with some more barbershop philosophy. He had all my old heads mad and cussing.

Jay?

You remember Jay. He used to cut hair here before he opened his own shop out North.

Jay, the McDonalds man?

Yep, I forgot all about that story. He was on another one today.

I am sure he was.

Hold up- here comes another customer. Let me buzz him in. Welcome to Vee's!

Aw, that's Breeze.

What up, Vee? My man, what up Trey? Sorry to hear about your father.

What up Breeze, appreciate that man.

Yeah, that really messed me up. My mom called while I was driving back into town and told me. I had to pull over on the side of the road, I was so down. Your pops was a real good dude. He always looked out and never judged me.

Thanks, Breeze.

No, for real, at least you got a dad to miss. I celebrated my 33rd birthday last Saturday. My dad hasn't once in those 33years told me happy birthday, but last week he called on the Sunday after my birthday. I thought maybe he was calling to finally say, "Happy Birthday, son." This man is gon' tell me, no lie, "You know my birthday was Friday. I can't get a call from my son." My father does not even remember my birthday was a day after his. That is crazy, but anyway, your pops was a real stand-up dude.

Dang Breeze…I appreciate that.

(barbershop collective)

Yea man sorry to hear about that. We didn't know your pops had passed.

It's cool, I did not tell y'all. Breeze knew because he knew my dad.

Were y'all close? If y'all were not, it does not matter anyway. That is not on you. Like Breeze said, that is on him. He the reason you here, it was his responsibility to have a relationship.

I feel you Big Zo, but me and my pops were good; that is some real talk though! Hey Vee, I am going to go to the back and wait for Rasheem in his chair. I will holla at you on the way out.

Alright, on your way out you got to refresh me on Jay's McDonald theory, too.

I got you. Look who just rolled up.

Ten Speed! Should I let him in?

Why wouldn't you?

You know he barely be taking baths. I am looking out for my patrons. Plus, it is too early for him to empty trash or sweep up anything.

Man, nobody is worried about Ten Speed. Everybody in the shop know him. Go ahead and buzz him in.

You right. What up, Ten Speed?

What up, Boss Man, Vee?

What are you sweating for? It is too early, and it is not even hot outside yet.

Boss Man, I have been riding all morning.

Riding where?

I am just getting in the city from Knoxville.

(barbershop collectively laughs)

Ten Speed, you know you did not ride your bike from Knoxville to Nashville. Especially not this morning.

Boss man, I promise, on everything I love. I left this morning, 5am.

10 speed it's eight-thirty in the morning. It is a four-hour drive in a car. You did not ride your bike.

Boss man no disrespect, you just cannot drive. I have been riding bikes since I was knee high. You did not start driving cars till you was 16. I got road experience. You just don't know all the tricks yet. Keep driving though; one day you might catch me.

(barbershop collective laughter)

Alight Ten Speed well, you are going to have to come back later. Barbershop has not been open long enough for the trash to be taken out or floors swept.

Okay, okay, I appreciate that Boss man, Vee. I will be back. But let me hold something.

No sir, Ten Speed, you don't ever comeback when I prepay. You're going to have to wait.

Come on Boss Man, I am good for it.

Ok, let me hold on to your bike, until you come back. You got to be tired of riding anyway.

Naw, boss man, see you think you funny. Me and my ten speed do not part ways. I heard you try to slide that slick little line about me being tired in there. I am telling you I rode from Knoxville this morning. As a matter of fact, take a look at this.

Man, I do not want to see no old newspaper.

It is not old.

Well, I don't need it. I am cutting hair.

Let me see it.

Yeah, Trey, here. You look at it. What kind of paper is it?

Ha, it is the Knoxville News.

Yeah right. What is the date?

Vee, you are going to trip. Its today's date.

(Collective laughter from barbershop)

I told you Vee, but don't worry. I will wait for my money when I come back and keep the paper youngblood. You gon' need something to read with all these people waiting.

(barbershop laughing)

Alright Vee, I am going to the back for real this time to wait on Rasheem.

Cool, you may want to call him, too. Just in case. You may be back there waiting, but at least Ten Speed left you something to read.

Ha, will do.

The Walk

I don't know what it is, but there is something about walking and thinking. As soon as I took my first step out of the barbershop, my mind took off like a dog finally off its leash, racing to every point of interest its owner had restricted it from going. I was a hound dog roaming freely in my mind as I sniffed around at anything entertaining. The old, buried bones of history garnered my attention, as I dug into the forgotten files of my memories. I was brought back to the last time I had to walk to a destination. It was about five years ago. My car was at the auto shop down the street from my parents' home. The shop called and said the car would be ready by noon. My mom was working from home the first part of the day, so she coordinated with my stepdad to pick my car up during lunch. The shop would be closed by the time I got off work. Thankfully, my sister was temporarily living at our mom's house, and although we worked for different companies, we shared the same parking lot. She offered to take me home after work, which was the absolute least she could do for her "brother," Major emphasis on the "least," which would be the theme of that particular evening. My mother always had this thing about borrowing and lending. She would say don't let people borrow or lend nothing. If you cannot give it away, then you do not have it to lend. She got this advice from Oprah, although if Oprah was speaking monetarily, this was easy advice to give. I doubt Oprah lacked the financial ability, but what about time? When it comes to other people's time, ninety-nine percent of people will give you the least amount of it. Hence my thought that the least my sister could have done was drop me off to get my car. The thing about doing the least, is that if you could do less you would. Doing the least is worse than doing nothing because it shows your heart's bank statement. It pulls back the robe of selfishness that you think doing the least covers. See, everything she was doing, she would have done if I was not with her. My car was on the same route she had to go, to get where she had to get. So, on the surface this was the perfect match for her to do the least and still get me what I wanted most. Unfortunately, the pot was just warming up, and that grain of salt offer to let me ride home with her was only slowing the surface boil.

It had been a while since we had been in the car together for any real length of time. I figured this could be a good time to check up and check in, but instead I was met with an uneasiness of awkward frustrations. Awkward because she was complaining about familiar traffic that she runs into every afternoon on her routine trip home. The huffs and puffs toward the stopping and going of traffic was befuddling. Like thunder on a clear day, I looked around like what could she possibly be mad about it. This is normal rush hour traffic. Behind the gasps of irritation, she would periodically say how she wanted to hurry up and get home so she could exercise. I have known my sister her entire life. So, I knew this was not my time to interject with optimism. Instead, I listened and observed, making sure not to say anything to rock the boat, but my mind was racing. I was thinking to myself, the only difference between today any other day is that I am with you." Nothing else- this is not a new way to go home; the traffic is no different than it is any other time. The only new variable to her perfect equation was me, the least of me, and it was about to get worse. Her frustration from the beginning of the ride home was only toward what I thought was regular rush hour traffic, but there was another impediment neither of us knew about yet. See, my car was at the shop ready to be picked up. The keys to my car were at the house. Moms was running late leaving the house, so the best she could do was pick up my car keys on the way to a board meeting and drop them off with my stepdad. My stepdad dropped off my keys at the house but left back out to go run errands. None of this was known to me until we pulled up to the house. I initially only thought my sister was picking me up from work and taking me home where my car was. As we pull into the driveway, she asked, "Where is your car?" I said, "I do not know. Let me call mom. Moms explained what happened and where my car keys were. The conversation was 2 minutes max. "I'll run in real quick grab my key, you don't even have to get out, and you can drop me off." I said casually. At the same time, she was already cutting off the car and grabbing all her stuff to go inside the house. I knew there was a chance she would do this, so I took it on the chin. I thought. After about an hour of waiting for her to finish exercising, I did the big no, no. I interrupted her workout, only to find out this was just the intermission and she had another forty-five minutes left. What I thought was a jab to the chin of adult patience, turned into a horse kick to the sternum as she pressed play and started back exercising. I was heated. My maturity could not help me find the level of understanding I needed to accept why my sister could not have drop me off really quick, or why she could not even ponder it. The shop was literally down the street. It was so close we used it as the final landmark when giving people directions to the house. It was at most an eight-minute drive max to the shop! As this climatic wave of emotions was nearing peak crest mom called to take it to new heights. She could not understand why I was still at the house. "Why are you still at the house?" she asked. "Your daughter wanted to exercise first before taking me to my car," I said. "Where are you? Are you close? You may be able to take me quicker than her," I suggested. "No, I am not close to being home. Both of you all are something else." "You all?" I asked. "Welp, you might as well spend the night. Ha, ha, ha."

It was her laughter as she trailed off the phone that sent me. It was doing me no service to be mad and do nothing. In my mother's house I had revolted back to childlike strategies. I was pouting. Sitting there mad, bubbling over when I could have moved on to a solution. Walk! It was the coldest night of the year so far, 2 degrees, but I was so heated that I welcomed it. Luckily when I moved out, I had left a winter coat, beanie, and some Timberland boots in my closet.

It is an empowering feeling to be able to walk where you want to go. Transportation by foot is a well-known secret that moves incognito in the non-transient south, where we are so dependent on a vehicle. Due to this, I never fully experienced the gift of walking. This gift of walking was celebrated by our parents when we took our first steps. Unfortunately, these first steps toward our independence quickly fade as attention and excitement moves to new milestones. Most importantly, the milestone of learning to drive. This achievement stifles your excitement, growth, and education of walking anywhere. In Tennessee, the rite of passage into adulthood is driven upon, and there are few sidewalks to be optioned. So, as I walked out of the house that cold winter night, I knew I had the ability to walk, but did not know the education on independence I would receive by walking. It was unexpectedly wonderful like an organic Saturday night. Not only did I not need my sister to take me to get my car, but my dependency on a vehicle was oversold and overhyped. I could walk to many of the places I drove to. This had never entered my mind until now. It was understood that cars are needed because we do not walk, but walking gave me a freedom I did not know was available. It was like getting to a secret level on video game and realizing you had been playing the game with constraints that confined your player. I imagine it was how Forrest Gump felt when he finally was able to run. A rush of excitement, that feeling of never wanting to be back in those braces, fueled his adrenaline to run with no regard. He felt free, for the first time in his life, all he needed was him. There could be no running for Forrest until he was independent of those braces. I recognized the Forrest Gump in me when I was learning to ride my bike. It was a black and gray BMX Bike with training wheels. Those training wheels did not teach me how to ride, they taught me how to ride with training wheels. Those training wheels taught how not to ride. They helped develop my balance and confidence to be independent. I remember the day I shed myself of those training wheels. I waited outside for my dad to get home from work. I ran to his car excitingly waiting for him to get out. He quickly got out of the car thinking something was wrong. "It's nothing wrong, I said. I just want you take my training wheels off before you go inside. I made him stay outside after he took them off, so he could watch me speed around the house over and over as the adrenaline raced through my legs. I was finally free, and the freedom of not needing assistance is dangerously empowering. My training wheels had taught me how to ride within the limits of their maker. Their limits being designed to keep the rider from falling. To be the rider's guiding hand of balance and safety, but now free from that assistance I could test these limits. I was free to ride and more importantly free to fall. What would happen if I found success in the fall zone? This is what the X Games are all about. People who have found freedom outside the restraints of general safety. This is the empowering danger of independent freedom. That exhilarating rush of endorphins that numbs the alarm in your comfort zone giving you this pseudo empowerment that you can do anything. In sports and other competitive aspirations pushing these limits is revered, but what about socially? I learned as a kid the social parameters of etiquette, but I know people, right or wrong, who have found success off the beaten path. When I walked out of my parent's house, I felt the power and freedom of finding success off the beaten path of social etiquette. Patience has always been a part of being socially aware/intelligent. I never thought as an adult I would be willfully operating in the area of impatience. Being impatient is a childish trait., always followed by a childish antic like attempting to run away. I threatened to leave a couple of times as a child because I did not get my way, but I never made it out of the driveway before thoughts of dependency magnetically pulled me back in to the house. Now my magnet had been flipped. I was independent and had my own magnetic field.

Those training wheels of patience were for my yesteryears, and I was enjoying this new level of freedom. Walking and wondering why I had waiting so long to test the limits as an independent. I had not felt this way since I hung up on a friend in college. Although foreign to me personally, hanging up on people seemed to be common practice. Common enough that it comes as no surprise to see and hear it happen to someone every day. I had been hung up on before, but I had never tried it. Shockingly, when I did, it affected me to a level of deviant embarrassment. I remember it so vividly because it was the first and last time I ever did it. It gave me an uncomfortable power, a feeling I felt this walk was giving me. In that moment, hanging up on my friend mid conversation was immeasurably pleasurable, but at

the same time it was a trashcan juice move. I
knew it was wrong because I had been teetering on
the fence of "should or shouldn't I" for the past
couple of what felt like half an hour. As I slowly
roller-coastered to the apex of this phone call, my
stomach full of monarchs, I disrespectfully belly
flopped like an inexperienced diver off a dirtbag
cliff landing in an ocean of remorse. It felt so
kingly to dismiss the conversation when I was
ready with no recourse. I had safely dived and
avoided all the jettisoned cliffs and rocks social
etiquette had warned me about. I had successfully
found safety in the danger zone. My years of time
with the training wheels of social norm always put
fear in me of doing something like this. It was like
a king saying, "Enough- off with your head." The
issue was I am no king. I am me, and "me" had to
decide who I wanted to be. It felt great. I never
knew I could silence someone's side of the
conversation because I didn't want to hear it. It
was so entitled yet gratifying. Entitled gratification
is a dangerous drug. Thankfully as I was coming
down, "Cinderella's clarity" came too. Unlike a
king and his circle of yes men that protect from the
ill speech of the malcontent against him, I could
not operate in X Games of social norms. I knew
the backlash that would eventually come from

being this kind of person was a weight I could not
bear alone and dismissing people when I felt like it
would lead to a lot of alone time. It would be the
equivalent an X Gamer wearing helmet, pads,
gloves, etc. in the anticipation that something will
go terribly wrong. I didn't want to live with that
type of social protection. I quickly came off my
high horse, as this was not a race I wanted to run
and called my friend to walk back my actions. That
high of accomplishment I felt to be able to
impatiently shut someone up completely was
amazing. In that moment, my actions were truly
speaking louder than my words. Fortunately, my
actions were too loud for me as well. This walk
was giving me that same gratification. The same
mentality that allowed me to hang-up on my friend
was the same thing that led me out the door. I was
done and my patience level on zero. I hung up on
the idea of anybody taking me to get my car. Part
of me felt wrong about it, like I should have waited
but the other side was enjoying this newfound
power. I was Frodo in the LORD of the Rings,
except this time it was LORD of the FEET, and the
more I walked, the more indignant I was
becoming.

I grew in prideful invincibility with every step. This cloak of protection allowed me to walk unaffected by any previous concerns I ever had about walking. The weather and loose dogs being my primary concerns. As the heat or ac blasted and unleashed dogs roamed their areas of ownership, I thankfully only had noticed these things from my car, but now out in these cold weather elements, my purposeful gait mixed with a swelling bravado was keeping me just as heated physically as I was mentally for having to be walking in the first place. As I lumbered along this snowless, terrain less, suburban street in my Timberlands, I quickly realized how foolish I was to own these boots. These boots were not meant for walking and my hips were alerting me to it. I felt like I was stomping the ground, my ergonomically friendly heel toe gait was being held captive in these boots, so I marched stomping toward my independence, and my militant mentality was perfectly suited for it. As I soldiered along, my body warmed and ready, I knew my second battle was two turns away on a dangerously steep hill. This hill was so steep, it was never traveled upon during snow and ice, leaving the residents who lived on the hill stuck until everything melted. It was even frowned upon to sled down this hill. There had been some terrible accidents that left kids with broken legs and arms, but snow and ice were not my concern tonight. It was Lassie. Lassie on the tv shows was friendly heroic dog/collie, but this collie, whose house I was approaching only wore sheep clothing. I had seen this dog numerous times chase, lunge, and bark at strangers as I drove by saying to myself, "I'm glad that is not me." Today it would be me, but I had a plan. Growing up I loved dogs, studied dogs, for a short time even thought I wanted to be a veterinarian. During my youthful interest of dogs, I remember reading and hearing that dogs could sense fear. Well tonight, there would be no smell of fear on me. I was too determined to prove a point to myself that I could walk to where I needed to go and I was not going to let a dog stop me. My sister's disregard for my patience had fueled me, so I would take my chances. My tune on the necessity of my Timberland boots quickly changed as I climbed the hill where Lassie lived. I knew they weren't meant for walking but these 12" steel toes boots would be incredibly useful for protecting me against ankle bites, kicking, and stomping if Lassie rushed after me. I crept toward his house looking for him as if I was the dog. We saw each other at the same time, and both of us froze. I did not freeze because I was scared, but prepared. I wanted to let him know I was ready if he was ready. He rested on his hind legs and watched as I continued to march away from his house. I turned and faced him as I descended the hill not giving him a chance to surprise me. I remembered reading in one of those dog books to never turn your back on dogs that may attack. I breathed a little easier as I came off the hill and on to flat ground. Although I was not even halfway to my destination, I felt accomplished. Those mountains of concerns I had about walking were now molehills. There were no more hills, no more loose dogs that I knew of. I was warm, and the rest of walk was pretty much a straight shot. I felt my stomping becoming less intense, as I came to at ease. My cloak of invincibility did not seem necessary as I relaxed my thoughts of any other impediments.

I was only two streets away from the car shop by now. Unfortunately, they were the longest stretches of my walk. As I was about to turn on to the first street, I quickly realized the lack of streetlights and the speed of the cars approaching. I was still on a residential street, but they were coming off a main road, and these late rush hour drivers had not yet adjusted to the slower 30 mile and hour speed limit. I knew this because I had often been guilty of this, too. I turned on to the street but decided to walk in the grass of the houses I was passing due to the lack of streetlights, speed of cars, and no sidewalks. I was a little over two miles from my next turn. Walking past these speeding cars, I began to reassess my risk of danger. I realized I had under analyzed my concerns of walking. The contrast between driving and walking was clearer now that I was doing it. Driving afforded me a protection I did not fully calculate. In my car there were protections, safety measures in place to prevent major concern while traveling along a residential street, but those were for vehicles only. Walking, I was my only protection and safety. I was the bumper, steel, aluminum, seat belt, air bag, etc. I was so caught up in the weather and the lassie's, that I forgot about Lassie's owner. Lassie's owner: the texter, the drinker, the speeder, the sleeper, the multitasker, the depressed, the drug user, the homeowner whose yard I was slightly walking in, and the occasional racist. The just because I can, I am going to yell 'Nigger' as I speed by. I know this city and its capabilities because I grew up here. The city that in my elementary school had 600 kids, and 15 of them were African Americans.

By high school, the student population quadrupled but percentages stayed the same. I knew this, but never thought about it. My parents did a great job of bearing the thick filmy substance of racism as I grew up. Aside from the police, driving while Black limited the opportunities of random racist acts, but walking while black with Timberlands on, a beanie, and a Phat Farm Eskimo style coat in Tennessee, on a dimly lit highly trafficked white American suburban street left me keenly aware of my vulnerability. I am sure the percentages of people driving by were more likely to be sober, a texter, a drinker, high, sleepy, or multitasking. I also knew they would be more likely to try to avoid hitting someone because regretfully, I had been all the other types of drivers in my life, but a racist, I could not account for their actions. I took my toboggan off, made sure my hood was not flailing up, trying to gentrify myself on the fly, in case someone called the police saying they saw a black man walking in their yard. I recalibrated my awareness radar to the level of a walking driver. Walking with the wisdom told to all new drivers, "You can't just drive for yourself; you have to drive for the drivers around you. Don't assume the other drivers are paying attention." My steps were led by this wisdom. I straddled the pavement road and the edges of people's yards unsure how they felt about a Black man walking slightly on their property, especially at night. It would have been safer to walk completely in their yards instead of tight roping that line of safety while cars zoomed pass. Each time a car would approach I would step all the way into the yards of the passing houses, then promptly start tight roping again. Appeasement is a weight all minorities bear in suburbia, and although these actions are a necessary precaution, this balancing act of pacification was getting old. I quickened my pace, anxiously anticipating getting off this road and to my final turn- a well-lit main street with lights and the unicorn of the south, also known as a sidewalk. As I came around the curve, I could finally see the traffic lights up ahead flashing like a lighthouse. I was nearing the last stretch. I made it to the main street intersection and let out a sigh of relief. No more straddling, I was finally on the sidewalk. Another 2 miles, and I would be at my car. The rush hour traffic was over, and the road had become surprisingly peaceful as herds of cars occasionally passed by. Tired of the cars' noises and talking to myself, I slipped my earphones on. I checked my surrounding before I turned the volume up; I knew my hearing would be deafened

by the music and did not want any surprises. I was
disappointed to turn around and see I was right to
look. It was a police car. Did someone call the
police about a Black man walking in their yard?
Maybe. Did a driver pass by call saying he saw a
strange man walking down the street? Perhaps. Or
was it a coincidence that a police officer just
happened to be driving down a main street at the
exact time I was walking? No matter the reason,
the slow stalk of this officer was uncomfortable.
He was traveling well below the speed limit. I was
not sure how long he had been behind me, but I
knew it did not have to be. I was not walking faster
than a car. In high school I briefly worked for a
drug store. The manager always preached about
acknowledging customers as they entered. He said
this deterred criminal's because you alerted them
that you saw them, so I decided I would
acknowledge the officer and let him know I saw
him. I turned around and waved him down. He
cautiously pulled up, "Excuse me officer is
Bridgestone up ahead on the corner? I'm headed
over there to pick my car up." He answered yes. I
said thank you, and he drove on by. It's funny how
the same tactic that works for criminals works for
a cop, but humans are humans, and
acknowledgement goes a long way.

Had my sister acknowledged my patience for her, I would have waited, but for her to continue about her regularly scheduled program as if I did not exist, gave me a freedom of obligation to do as I wished with no regard or explanation as to why. Thanks, or maybe no thanks to her, I finally reached my car.

Falling or Landing?

For the past eight days I had purposely not
acknowledged my father's passing. The memories
of him left me fixated as they ran rampant through
the shelves of my brain. Since the time I had found
out he had passed, my body instinctively went into
shock. I took my hands off the wheel and let auto
pilot kick in, but now it was time to land. The pilot
woke me from my thoughts and advised we were
preparing for descent. Please put tray tables up and
fasten seatbelts. We will be coming down through
the tail end of a storm and there may be some
turbulence. Great, turbulence! I hated flying. I
hated taking off. I hated landing, but mostly I
hated turbulence. I had been flying high above the
storm, on a row all to myself, as I occasionally
lifted the blind to look out the window and gaze at
the clouds. Just as I was getting used to this cloud
nine flight, a jolt of imbalance reminded me why I
was on the plane in the first place. It was time for
me to fully process my father's death. I knew the
descent to acceptance would be bumpy and
stomach dropping at best. Once I started to accept
that my memoires of him, were memories, the
wheels would drop, the wings would lower, and
Father's Airline Flight 101318 would land, but not

without turbulent emotions. Emotions I had never experienced and did not want to deal with, but it was time for me to face those feelings like it was time for me to face my fear of heights by walking the bridge.

Unlike my last walk, I had on the proper shoes this time, but I could not get away from marching. This time it was a mental march. My cadent approach of left, left, left, right left, hypnotized me from the gut checking battle I was walking towards. A battle I had inherently stayed away from my entire life, so I could not leisurely walk towards that bridge. Leisure affords an allowance that I can get to it as I please. I had been pleased to stay away from facing the fear of heights my entire life, so mentally I had to march. See, you can march and be afraid. The military exemplifies that. Marching is a part of their basic training, instilling order and direction as a habit of survival. Those who served during war times likely received a fresh reminder every day that death was happening around them. That had to be a fearful time, and when fear is present you naturally do not walk into it. Your steps are measured with an awareness of your fear. The only way to walk in the direction of fear is with measure, and to walk with measure is to march. So, I commanded myself to march and see what this fear was all about.

Heights had always been an obstacle for me. It did not matter where the height was coming from, a window seat on an airplane, riding over a bridge, or staring out of a skyscraper- they were all the same to me. If free falling was a possibility, I was scared. I remember when I was young waking up in the middle of the night in a sweaty thankfulness- thankful the bed had finally caught me from my endless free-falling dream. Over the years, I had tried to overcome my fear of heights with maturity, but my fight or flight instincts were too strong for my aged reason. I assumed everyone had experienced the fear of falling, even birds. Birds with wings made for flying are scared. I have watched many National Geographic shows where the mother bird leaves the nest, urging their baby's initiation into birdhood and to enjoy the skies. What is interesting is when a baby bird first builds the courage to finally attempt to fly, it does not. The bird's inches closer to the ledge, flaps it wings, and falls. During the fall, the baby bird learns the most important lesson of its life and with that lesson strips away the fear of falling forever. The baby learns to land. My nightmare of

endlessly falling could have been a sweet dream if
I had ever thought to myself all I have to do is
land. If I can land, I will not die, which is the real
reason I was afraid of heights. Heights were an
opportunity for death, and I was afraid to die until
the recent death of my father. My father had fallen
suddenly.

The baby bird learning that falling was a part of
life turned out to be more important than flying.
Learning how to land was essential to the 'how' of
flying. If you can't land, you should be afraid of
flying. Landing is simply a prepared fall. You
can't be fearful of heights if you are prepared to
land. When people consider a favorite
superpower, they often choose the ability to fly;
why not choose landing? Landing is the
overlooked superpower. Imagine being able to fall
from any height and know you will land safely.
The greatest gift God gave birds is landing, but I
had been living focused on the flight. I thought if
straightened up and flew right that I would descend
and not fall. I ignorantly thought that's how life's
descension worked. Descending brings with it the
expectation that you are in control.   The baby
bird's first attempt to fly was no descent to the
ground, but a fall and landing. God allows some to

descend to old age while others fall with time remaining on the clock. Too busily occupied in the sky of life, I had not paid thoughtful attention to all the fallen around me. My father falling unexpectedly, was Lasik surgery to how I saw the heights in my life. Like a baby bird, my parents had taught me early how to land spiritually. My landing was Jesus. Everyone will fall or descend to death, but Jesus is how you safely land. Like birds, the belief of how to land in my family had been passed down for generations, but spiritually, I was in the sky ignorantly thinking I control how and when I would come to land with Jesus. My entire life heights had reminded me I was not in control of that. If I fell, I would likely die. The fear of death was so strong I forgot about my belief in spiritually landing. I was like that baby bird on the ledge for its first attempt at flying, nervously inching toward the edge, scared of what would happen if I fell only to realize by falling, the worst thing that could happen, is I would land. Not die, but land.

Land as my father landed.

That's what I said to myself as I looked over the bridge. My stomach stayed in place for the first time in my life. Hypnotized by the waves and ripples created by the barges that methodically powered by, I looked intently at the water without losing my stomach in fear. I reconciled with my fear now, knowing the worst thing that could happen was I land. Examining the distance between the water and the bridge, not afraid to fall anymore, was unshackling. I was not sure when I told my sister a couple of days ago, while picking out my father's burial plot, "I don't think I'm afraid to die anymore." During that conversation I was still gathering my thoughts and speaking from a fresh wound of pain and shock, but now standing on the bridge I was contemplating with more clarity what I meant. My father fell and knew how to land safely. He had taught and showed me how to land, so why fret the fall? Fretting will not stop a thing.

So, I stared into the depths of the fall, ready to land.

I had faced my fear, and finally it turned away from my stare.

Accomplished, I walked toward the end of the bridge. I noticed on that end the security fencing had stopped short of the bridge's railing. I squeezed between the railing and the fencing. I stood there with no security fencing or railing to separate me from facing my defeated arch nemesis. All these years heights had been the mouse to my elephant. It was the uncomfortable fear that frightened me to my core, but now the feeling was gone.

I stood victorious but with a tinge of shamefulness as I peered over the edge fully confident. Shameful that it took death for me to truly see the fragility of life and accept that I cannot run from it. Crossing over to the other side of that fence, leaving comfort and confidence behind I faced my fear, only to realize that a fear faced puts everything back in its familiar comfortable place. That discovery was embarrassing- that something so small as heights had stifled me. The elephant in me had finally seen the mouse as a mouse, and I was free from falling.

I wish I could explain what happened next. They say pride comes before the fall, so I could not have fallen. I had no pride as I looked over the edge of the cliff into the river. How could I find the emotions to boast over an accomplishment that was fueled from the loss of my father? I had only walked as a dedication to him, and I would walk it all back and live with fear of heights forever for him to be alive. I was emotionally weightless, like fruit in Jell-O, too stuck in this new mental space to leap.

 Everything was still processing for me.

I had no pride for a fall, nor the lows for a jump. All I know was the natural compass provided by the instinctive feelings of fight or flight had hidden their hand as I speedily surrendered into the strength of gravity's arms.

If you have ever experience jumping onto a waterbed, only to realize it's nothing like the pool you imagined it would be, that smack, that sudden stop in motion you felt is not even a distant cousin to the impact I felt. There was not a piece of my body that did not collapse from the velocity with which I hit the water. I hit the cement skin of the water and my body surrendered. Within the depths of the river there was nothing to muster, no second wind to grasp for. Not even a futile attempt of adrenaline was present in my body to help me survive. Somewhere in the abyss I hung paralyzed in the eddy of consciousness. Unable to give the entertaining theatrics of fighting to survive, I had seen so often in movies, I motionlessly floated. As consciousness neared the curtain call, my senses started to bow out. First my sight, followed by taste, touch, and hearing. As smell entered the stage, I knew it was time. I knew once I inhaled, it would be my last, for to smell the water while in water would mean my end. As I fatefully breathed in, to my surprise there was no water. My expected gurgled drowning was substituted for a muffled breath of air. Although I had breathed deep, the air faintly came in like sipping through a broken straw, but a broken straw when you are thirsty will always satisfy. Lacking all my other senses, I could not identify how I was breathing. "Am I dead?" I asked. Confused, I used the only sense I had left, my sense of smell. As I breathed in, I attempted to smell with the intensity of a blood hound, no scent came. Like "Beautiful Mind," I covered my cognitive chalkboard with every possible solution, but none balanced the equation. I was down to the nubs of my mental chalk, physically beat and now perplexed in confusion. The questions remained. How am I still breathing? The anxiousness of wanting to know what was going on, would not let me calm down and just breathe. The more I smelled, the less I enjoyed my befuddled ability to breathe. I racked my brain for answers until I fell asleep, or until I woke up. Without my other senses I could not tell the difference between the two. "Am I in hell? This must be hell, I said. I am in hell! I am in HELL!"

Memorable Breath

Calm down.

Who said that?! How can you hear me?!

You are not in hell. If you must ask yourself are you in hell, then you are not. Just as heaven is unimaginably perfect and virgin to any human experience, there is also not a word in your Webster filled brain that needs to reason what is hell. You will know hell without an introduction and heaven without a hello.

Who are you?

"Who am I?" You ask. Have you given up on your initial question? The question which led you to think you were in hell. How are you breathing? Behind that answer, I am sure are many questions. I could answer all of them, but with all answers you must show your work. Your questions, your work, your answers, but I do not mind being a compass as you search. You have log jammed your brain with the same question, how are you breathing? I will not repeat the true, but overused "insanity definition," but how about trying a different approach? Have you ever thought about the why? Why are you breathing?

What? I know why I breathe. I need air to live. I need it to survive. What kind of question is that? I breathe for the same reason you do.

Yes, we breathe for the same reason, but that is not what I asked you. I asked you why you are breathing. Maybe these simple "1 + 1 = 2" type questions are too easy, and you already knew you needed air to survive. Why are you in a place where there is no air for you to survive? 1 + 0 = 2, That is not adding up. Did you want to live?

Yes, I was looking over the river and I guess I slipped.

You slipped? Ok well, if I had slipped into an equation that I was not supposed to solve and somehow got the right answer, I would not have been worried about the "how" part as much as celebrating the fact that I had the answer. Why aren't you celebrating breathing?

All I know is that I slipped, and I'm here.

You slipped? You slipped into a bad situation, which right now isn't that bad, and you want to know why? It's not bad because you are breathing.

Slipped, fell, jumped, whatever. I am here.

Why? If you jumped, why would you have jumped?

I do not know. I guess, I was not afraid to fall. I was okay to land.

Land? What do you mean okay to land?

I was okay with dying, landing.

Gotcha, so you are here, stuck, but ready to land, wondering how you have not landed, instead of why. The answer to "how" gives reason, but the answer to "why" gives purpose. And purpose would have kept you from slipping.

What are you talking about? I am somehow alive, but lifeless which is strange, listening to you, a stranger in strange place talk about how versus why. I thought you offered to be my compass. Could you please just point me in the right direction?

A compass does not choose destinations. It shows direction toward that destination. Until you know where you are and where you want to go, there is nowhere to guide you. Even If I pointed you in a direction you cannot see, so give me a chance. I am all you got.

Alright.

Alright, what is the purpose of you breathing?

I have never thought about breathing. I have always done it.

Well, you don't seem to be going anywhere. Think about it now. Think about breathing. Tell me the last time you took a memorable breath.

Ummm…a memorable breath? Ok.

It had to be around the time I was moving back from college. I had been in Minneapolis for school. As graduation neared and my return home approached, I was in the hunt for a job. I had persistently been calling all my connections, but none were coming through. In my life when nobody else could come through for me, my mom always did. It was no different this time. As always, she had been sitting back observing me as I spun my silk from Minneapolis to Nashville crafting my spider web of opportunity, sure to catch a job. As my homecoming neared, my web of resources still had not caught a job. As the numbers in my zip code changed, so were numbers in my bank account. My checking account was moving south faster than I had, and after weeks of web vibrations only to find out they were all just wind, mom stepped in. She said, "I know you're still looking for jobs and waiting to hear back from some of them, but you know it's nothing wrong with taking a job to get you by until then. We just had a position open in the laundry department at the Nursing Home. It's third shift, but it is something. I can make a call." A younger me would have turned my nose up at working a laundry job, but mom knew the right time to offer me a fly. My web was more cobweb than spider web, so I was appreciative of anything other than the dust my pockets were collecting.

My first day working that job was a hot, stagnant, muggy summer day. The laundry room was in the basement. The air didn't work, and there were no windows. The morning shift would crack the exit door which led to dumpsters until the sun went down, to help with air ventilation. Security did not allow for us to keep them open at night due to the neighborhood, but the stench of the clothes and linen were more of a "DO NOT ENTER" sign than the deterrent of any campus security. On the days the sun was out, it would shine bright through the exit doors making it hotter, baking us in the breath of summer heat. There was nothing like getting your shift started with the aroma of geriatric feces and sickness. I would often look at the particles floating through the sunlit air as I clocked in, praying my immune system did not call out today. The convection of smells that incensed the laundry room were face-changing. Just as a smile is a universal show of happiness, the smells in the laundry room created a universal grimace among my coworkers. Although the younger me figuratively would have turned my nose up at the job, the literal me had no choice but to turn my nose up. "Can't you smell that?!" I asked one of my coworkers. The smell some days was intolerable, and there was not a mask strong enough dilute it. The nurses kept a steady stream of dirty saturated linen baskets flowing to the basement as I am sure, they were happy to leave with us. My mom called me after my first week to see how I was doing. Hesitant to complain and wanting to show my gratitude, I stuck to thanking her for getting me in the door. During that conversation I learned that my mom did not even know where the laundry department was located which I completely understood because the nursing home made sure you could not just wander to the basement. There was only one elevator that led to the basement and you needed a code to descend to that "forgotten place." The basement was the solitary confinement for all odors in the nursing home, and the owners wanted to make sure that if the odors snuck out, they could only sneak out of the building toward the dumpsters and not up on to the floors. You must understand, in a nursing home odor is your first alert. My mother said on many occasions, "If you walk into a nursing home and smell urine or heavy bleach, be concerned for the residents. Somebody is likely not getting the proper care." Down in the basement, I would have loved to just be able to smell urine and bleach. Bleach would have been a sweet perfume in comparison to the foul odor of soiled linen. I worked the 3rd shift with two and half ladies: Bri, Ms. Linda, and Ms. Jackson. Linda was the half lady. She came in during 2nd shift and got off a couple hours into mine. Linda was in her mid-50's and had worked in the laundry department for 20 years. I stood frozen in disbelief as she told me she had been in the laundry department that long. I thought about the money we were making, divided by the smell, and multiplied it by twenty years. It totaled to modern day slavery. Hearing her story brought up a buffet of emotions from anger to thankfulness. Angry she had been working in the basement "septic tank" this long in the same position, yet thankful for this motivating, yet humbling experience. I say experience because there was no way I would allow it to be more than just that. Every day I tried to make her last two hours with me the easiest of her shift, just letting her fold the clean clothes. Clean clothes were the finish line of the "breathe and touch as little as possible marathon" in the laundry room. Bri and Ms. Jackson were like me in that they worked with the light at the end of the tunnel. Ms. Jackson had picked up a second job to help with her daughter's tuition. Her daughter only had 3 more semesters, and she said she would be done with the laundry. Bri was the youngest of all of us. She was 20 in Cosmetology School, working at Walgreens, and working with us in the nursing home. She would come to work either from school or Walgreens in full zombie mode. Her youth was the light at the end of her tunnel. She got minimal sleep during the week, so every break and lunch she would fall into a coma. She always said, "Make sure I don't oversleep." I looked forward to Bri working because she always wore some type of Bath and Body works type spray. Her smell lingered like a skunk spray from a Febreze can. I have heard of those romantic descriptions of being intoxicated by the smell of a love interest. I was in no way in love with Bri, but her smell had me intoxicated. Her scent would numb my senses as I drunkenly carried on the task of toilet work. I say toilet work because ninety- eight percent of everything I touched and inhaled would have been flushed down the toilet, but it was done in bed sheets, comforters, and pillowcases.

Once you finished washing and drying 3 or 4 loads, you would move to the folding table where all clean clothes were folded. Compared to everything else in our work area, the folding table was a big white clinical stain in the middle of the laundry room. That table was like a mirage in the desert; it was unbelievable to think there was anything down in the basement that could be this clean and white. The table was cleaned hourly, and it was frowned upon to even lean on it. It was the unicorn in the zoo of dirty laundry and was treated as such. When enough loads had been folded and were ready to be taken to the floors, each one of us would choose a floor to replenish with sheets, pillowcases, and blankets. The fourth floor always needed to be restocked the most. The residents on the fourth floor were the most dependent patients, and the fourth floor also housed the contagious wing. Nobody ever voluntarily took this floor, but not for those reasons already mentioned. It was for the same reason you never wanted to wash the fourth-floor laundry. The smell of death gifted to us in nicely wrapped biohazard bags came from that floor. You opened those bags with the uneasiness of clipping the right wire in one of those bomb movies. I would take a deep breath before opening, hoping to minimize the blast from the fourth-floor bag of surprise. When the residents had soiled the sheets really badly, the techs were supposed to rinse the sheets off before putting them in the bags. This rarely happened, leaving you with bedding embedded with chunks, mounds, mush, pebbles, balls, sand, and other textures of bodily waste. The smells waited excitedly, anticipating jumping out of the caked sheets of waste to tattoo their smells into our nostrils. Surprisingly, these smells are what led me to volunteer to take the fourth floor. "Are you sure?" the others asked. My first couple of weeks one of the ladies always handled the fourth floor because it took the longest to restock, and my speed wasn't efficient yet. "Yes," I said. The smell made me curiously mad. How could it be like this every day. The old childhood saying, whoever smelt it, dealt it. Well, I had smelt it and felt it. It was time I see who dealt it.

4th floor, going up. Ding. The elevator door sounded as it opened to the fourth floor. The smell rushed into the elevator like it was running away from something smacking me in my face, yet again. As I stepped out of the elevator on to the floor, it was warm, almost toasty. The smell was stronger and more potent, but worse than that, it was all encompassing. I was walking in the belly of the beast. As I searched for all the odorous offspring's parents, nobody was in their room. Occasionally I would see two feet at the end of a bed as I walked by but not enough culprits to explain the crime on my nose. The smell increased and the potency became stronger as I neared the end of the hallway. I turned the corner and my heart dropped. My nose had led me to a "Barack Obama length voting line" of residents waiting to be helped. As I walked past the doorways of the rooms, residents would see me and start asking for help. "Can you help me?" some would ask as they scooted in their wheelchair to the frames of the door. Others would groan or yell help repeatedly. "What do you need?" I asked. Every one of them needed to use the restroom. It all made sense now. Their sheets, pillowcases, blankets, and gowns were finally explained. I was not sure if legally I could help them being that I was just a laundry guy. Morally I wanted to but also did not want to do something detrimental to them or me. As I moved up the hallway passing the line of people waiting to be assisted to the bathroom, there was a lady with no legs sitting in her wheelchair. Unable to hold herself she had defecated in her chair. With sad, wandering eyes she looked up at me and then back down to show me what she had done. Pass the point of embarrassment, she was pushing it out onto the floor with her hand. Until her, I had told each patient the same thing. "I will go get help," and they all replied the same way, "Why can't you help me? You help me." She was unable to ask, but her defeated eyes said it all. I moved my cart of clean linen to the side of the hallway and grabbed the handles of her wheelchair. To sit helplessly in a chair of your own waste and wait unable to not smell it was too much. My heart raced as I wheeled her down the hallway looking for help. Help, I assumed, was the nursing station. To my dismay the nursing station was where the line started. There was no one I could notify- they all knew. All the nurses and techs knew there was a line. There was no urgency in their actions to make me feel otherwise. Some were working and assisting the patients, others were on break, going on lunch, or talking on the phone. Maybe T.V.

doctor shows had fooled me, but the hallway long line I had just passed, was an "all hands-on deck" line. Their laundry got quicker attention than they did. I frequently had to skip breaks or go to lunch late due to all the floors bringing down the dirty laundry at the same time, knowing we had to have those loads cleaned by next shift. We had a triage for their laundry, but not the patients. Looking at that long line, I now fully understood my grandparents and parents saying, "Whatever you do, do not send me to a nursing home." I often shared with my mom my hopes and dreams that I wanted to pursue. On one occasion I was running into some roadblocks and venting to her about it. After a brief encouraging endorsement, she said, "Know this-nobody is going to work your dream, like you, so don't be walking around here pouting because people not helping you. It's your dream." That fourth-floor scene embodied that. Nobody is going to work for your parents, grandparents, and love ones the way you do. Their yours. Those nurses and techs had a cutoff switch for those residents. It was a job, and they treated it that way. I'm sure there were some nurses and techs that went beyond the call of duty, but if all they did was do their job, it would look like what I witnessed. I unassumingly wheeled the lady to the front of the line and quietly told them there was a long line of people that need assistance but emphasized that this lady may need to be next. Thank you.

 I finally got around to stocking the linen closet and headed back down the hallway. As I entered the elevator and descended back to the basement any waiver or grandiose thought I had about it being better at some point for my parents to be in nursing home than at home with love ones vanished on that floor. There was only 30 minutes left till we got off. The television was blasting, drowning out the washers and dryers as Bri and Ms. Jackson started working on some of first shift's linen. The television was our apple in front of the horse that kept us going. That perk was adoringly highlighted during my orientation by the supervisor. Lowlighted was the fact you would be so busy you would have no time to enjoy it. Like a runner racing down the home stretch looking up at the monitor to see if any racers are close, I looked up to see what was on. It was on the movie "The Help." I jokingly thought to myself how fitting.

For someone who did not want to talk, you had a lot to say. I wish you could have seen your face when you talked about those smells. They must have lingered in your memories. Your facial expressions were so bad, they made me frown up.

Out of that whole story all you took from it was being entertained from my facial expressions towards smells.

Are you done with the story?

Yes, I am done. I talked for a long time.

Then yes, all I got from it were the faces you were making. They were so strong and exaggerated. They told a story your words could not. Anyway, that was your experience. You lived it. What did you get out of the story? I know where I am in my story. I know why I breathe. What did you get from your story?

Listen

You probably weren't even listening. A teacher told me two signs of a good listener are eye contact and nodding of the head to the speaker while they talk. Neither of which I know you did, since I cannot see. You did not do anything the whole time, no noise, no nothing. Even a preacher gets an amen every now and then.

So, you were preaching to me? If so, you would not get an amen out of me because you do not know the amen of your own story. The reason I did not do anything was because the whole time you were telling your story I was listening. Your teacher should have taught you the number one sign of listening- shut up. Shut up and listen. That is the reason you can tell a whole story about breathing and not know the why of it. You got to shut up when you talk.

What?! What type of sense does that make?

Listen when you speak. You already gave the answer of why you breathe, but you have not shown your work. It's because you have not shown your work that you cannot recognize the "why" in your story. Like I said from the beginning- its your problem; I will guide you along the way, but I will not solve it. Do not mistake my quietness for disinterest. My interest is undivided. I will make a noise when you go astray. If you are searching for affirmations when you speak, get them from yourself. You are so busy listening for me you cannot hear yourself; an amen from a sinner could just as easily be the boy who cried wolf, preacher. Listen when you speak, and you will hear your own answers.

Who is preaching now?

Even now you do not listen. You are so distracted by what you cannot do, you only hear. Have you never just listened to somebody? Not hearing, while thinking of a response. Just simply listening. No agenda but to listen. When you listen with a map, communication gets lost. You cannot determine the destination of someone's conversation. That is their verbal journey. Walk behind and follow. Then you will hear when to walk beside them. It is like listening to music; you let the musician take you on their journey. Your only job is listening. When you listen like that, you get the message. Have you ever listened with a blank slate?

Yes, and I think I know what you mean. I had been working that laundry job for about a month and was looking for something different. The sickness and disease coming down the laundry chutes was starting to weigh on me. I felt my immune system was at its wits end. Mom came through as always; she found me a way out. There was a nurse she worked with whose husband worked at a Call Center for hospital billing. Now, I am not an extrovert, rarely talked to strangers, and I hate bill collectors, but they were hiring, and I could not have been more thrilled to apply. I put my two-week notice in before I even had my interview. I knew I was leaving, leaving for fresh air and ventilation.

Waiting in the lobby of the Call Center, I did not have a clue what I was getting into, but I knew from the smell and the cool air conditioning it was already better than what I was doing. I had a lot of dogs growing up, but the best dog I ever had was Rosie. Rosie was a mutt, left in a box at a grocery store. Someone found her and took her to local veterinarian. They were going to send her to the pound, but they remembered my mother had just brought our dog Smokey in the day before. Smokey had gotten hit by a car and ending up

dying. The vet called my mom, saying they had a
puppy someone left at the grocery store and
wanted to know if she wanted to take it before they
sent it to the pound. Mom brought Rosie home
that same day. Rosie outlived every dog we had,
never ran away, and was always your best friend.
Rosie even got hit by a car and recovered fully. I
imagine Rosie walked into the house the way I
walked into to that lobby, looked around and knew
this was better than what she was doing.

You asked me, "Have I ever listened with a blank
slate?" I learned all about listening while working
at the Call Center. The job was simple on paper.
Patients call in to inquire and pay on their bills.
When they are not calling in, we are calling out.
Nothing tough about answering the phone; I have
been doing that my whole life, but I never
answered a phone with predetermined scripts.
This was not a regular phone call. I had a script.
Actors have scripts and play characters. Good
actors know their scripts and can play their
characters. After my first 30 days taking calls, I
knew my script by heart. I knew all my questions I
had to ask before the patient got off the line to
keep quality assurance and my supervisor off my
back. Yet and still, I was not collecting much

money, and collecting money was the name of the game. I got paid a decent hourly wage, especially if I include, I was not in the laundry room, but your real money came in when you were hitting your collections goals. That is when the bonus money kicked in. I guess the bonus money was the apple in front of the horse at the Call Center. I struggled collecting. I was not good at asking someone to pay their bill. I knew they owed, but I was not comfortable asking people for money. I made most of my money on inbound calls, but outbound calls, forget it. If it were an inbound call with questions, I could forget about getting their money after I answered their calls. They always answered with, "No I will mail it, I'll call back Friday, or I will pay it at the hospital." No matter the reason the result was still the same. Every week they would post collection totals to keep you abreast of percentage to goal. In my training class, there was only one person who was hitting goal every week. Some days he made so much money, he would transfer some of his payment calls to other reps to help them reach goal. I talked to some other reps that were in my training class during lunch about their collections, and they had noticed the same thing. No matter the time of day or the direction of the call, Greg from training was always making money.

One day I asked Greg, how he did it. Did you come from working at hospitals? Did you work insurance before you got here? What is your secret? He told me, "You got to listen. If you listen, you will hear when to ask for the money." He told me before working in the call center, he used to sell cars. Told me he sold ten cars in one day because he listened. He said, "I hear you on the phone. You sound like a robot. You follow the script to the tee, but every call is not the same. If you listen, you will know where to go." It was like I was in one of those old martial art movies and the grandmaster was teaching the young grasshopper. I had often listened to his calls, but all I gathered was that he was smooth on the phone. Patient paying, he is smooth. Not paying, he is smooth. Upset, he is smooth.   He does not know an answer- you got it… he was still smooth. As for me, patient paying, nervous. Not paying, very nervous. Question I cannot answer, extremely nervous. I figured if I knew the script, I would know what to say and not be nervous. Saying this to you now sounds even more silly than it did when I was attempting it. It is no different than being in a relationship and knowing it is over. You can know the words to say and still be nervous when you recite them because you do not know how it will be received. That was my issue, I spent so much time learning the script and hitting my prompts that I never listened.

I didn't listen because I did not know where the call would go if you did not play along with the script, so I waited. I waited but did not listen. I waited for the caller to stop talking, so I could recite my next line. Greg was right; I was robotic. I was treating my script like a monologue, not caring about anything but reciting my lines. Although a good actor knows their lines so well, they can play their character, a great actor knows the story so well they are the character. This allows them to have genuine off script dialogue without losing who they were cast to be. This was why Greg was so smooth. He knew the script so well because he understood what the author of the script was aiming for. He could have a nice, friendly game of verbal tennis, smoothly volleying the conversation, listening for the right time to get the money without losing the love. Greg was a collector, and the secret to collecting was listening. I took his advice and started to listen to each caller.

Listening made my nerves go away. I became the finger that your brain sends a message to when you need to pick something up. I listened attentively waiting to hear what I needed to do, blank slate listening. I started to hear what the patient was saying. The script was the DNA of the character I was playing, not a bunch of rigid lifeless responses I could not humanize. I learned how to become smooth and, in the process, never failed to reach the monthly goal and get my bonus again. It was learning to listen that quickly changed my fate and hierarchy in the Call Center.

I had been working at the call center now for 8 months, and I was getting bonus with my eyes closed. I still could not believe the key to achieving goal was all about listening. My supervisor would often remind me to keep it up. He said, "After a year with the company I could potentially move you up if there are openings." I did not need my new and improved listening skills to recognize this was just an overused monologue every supervisor in the Call Center was scripted to say. Even if my supervisor sincerely wanted me to have a better position, he had no power to make it happen, but fate did. I had recently applied to a heavily sought-after trainer position within the company, and fate had been slow cooking me and getting me seasoned ever since. During a monthly review of my job performance, my supervisor told me I was doing a good job and asked had I seen any new job listing for our department. I told him about the trainer position I was thinking about applying for. He let me know I likely would not get a response due to my seniority in the company and overall inexperience but to apply anyway. A couple days after I had applied for that training a position, I got a call. I work in a Call Center; all I do is get calls, but you must understand being a rep in the Call Center is like playing the slot machines. You click "GET NEXT CALL" and wait. You wait, hoping there is money on the other end of the line. Some days you hit; other days you go broke. That day fate called in. It was a Wednesday.

Fate was a 77-year-old woman from Florida, and she was defeated. As she spoke, she did her best to dam her emotions as she explained she was still at the hospital with her husband and had missed a call from this number. I advised her that it likely was a call about an open balance with the hospital. She said her husband had slipped and hit his head on the sink and bathroom floor, causing a severe brain injury. He was rushed to the hospital where they performed surgery and was now in a coma. She was confused that the hospital was even calling her considering she was still there waiting for her husband to come out of his coma. I told her to hold one second while I checked to see why we called. I did not see any open balance for her husband, but I did find a $50 balance in her name. I advised her that we did not call for her husband but for her. She had an unpaid copay for an ER visit, and the dam opened. She lost it. "I knew it! I was outside of my husband's room crying and the nurse kept trying to get me to go with her. I told her I was fine. I was just sad and worried about losing my husband. I told that nurse I did not want or need any help. She kept asking and asking. She told me they weren't going to charge me! This is wrong!" she exclaimed. "Just last year I lost a son and a daughter. They were murdered in a break in. I have one more daughter, but it is just me and my husband living in Florida. If he dies, I do not know what I'm going to do. Now you are charging me $50. I told that nurse I did not need anything. She came back with another nurse insisting I go downstairs and talk to somebody. They took me to the ER, but I could not understand why. Wouldn't you be crying and sad

if you were going through this? I did not need the
ER! I told them I was fine and went back upstairs
with my husband. I cannot believe the hospital
would bill me for this. My other daughter is
supposed to be here Friday. Well, when she gets
to the house, she is going to find a letter and me
dead on the floor. I am just going to kill myself.
It's just too much. I'm going to kill myself!"

Truthfully, until she said she was going to kill
herself, I was stealthily listening for the right time
to get that $50 from her. After 8 months, the Call
Center had turned me into a money chasing
assassin. The tears and sob stories did not move
me from taking a shot at a payment. I was going
to shoot for the money no matter what. It was
always conveyed by your supervisors that they
could be lying, but when she said she was going to
kill herself all that money talk disappeared. As she
spoke those words I started talking to
God. Nervously I asked, please tell me what to say.
I had never experienced anything like this in my
life. I waited for her to finish, not wanting to cut
her off. I said ma'am you cannot kill yourself. It
sounds to me like you are the rock of the family.
You are the one that's been holding the family
together, taking care and looking after your

husband, consoling your other daughter through the loss of her siblings; you are necessary. I know some weeks in Florida it rains, rains, and rains all day. At least it did for me every time I went to Disney World when I was a kid. We would not leave the park. My parents would buy us ponchos and rain gear. We would put it on and keep marching. Well right now you are in a rainstorm and I need you to put on your rain boots, poncho, and grab your umbrella, and keep marching. You already know this, but the rain will not last forever. Your daughter is going to be there on Friday. You got to be there too, so you both can be there for your husband. Do not worry about the $50 bill. I will get that taken off for you, so do not worry about that. I am going to call you back to check on you later today alright.

Yes, sir she said. Thank you very much.

No problem, I will talk to you soon. I stood up not sure what had just happened and told my coworker next to me I think I just helped somebody not commit suicide. What?! Did you tell your supervisor? No, I just got off the phone. Dummy you're supposed to tell your supervisor when you get a call like that. Huh? Yeah, your supposed to email your supervisor while you are on the phone or as soon as you get off go immediately to your supervisor. That is an emergency call. True, but I was not thinking about emailing nobody right then. So, I went to tell my supervisor what had happened. As soon as I told him what happened he started to move urgently. Still trying to figure out what just happen, I walked back to my desk.

The next day I came to work I had an email from my supervisor asking me to come to his office. He told me that management listened to the call. He said they always listen to threating calls, whether to others or themselves. I was nervous because I had told her one lie, white lie, but a lie still. I told her I would have her $50 bill cleared for her. It was a lie, but it was for the betterment, so I hoped I was not going to get in trouble for it. I knew when I said it, I was lying, but if all else failed I would pay for her $50 bill. To my surprise they said nothing about it. My supervisor told me management was impressed and pleased with the way I handled the call. When I got back to my desk, I had received 3 other emails from the "higher ups" all thanking me for how I handled the call. They were just names to me, as I had never met any of them, and I doubt they could pick me out of a line up; they were strangers saying thank you. I replied to all of them with a generic "no problem" type response. I was just being human. The next day was pay day Friday, and all I could think about was how I was going to spend it. I was walking down the hallway of the office suite when I heard an unfamiliar voice say a familiar name. I turned around to see a lady I had never seen before. "Hello I'm Natalie Wolfe. I heard your call the other day. You did an incredible job. I am glad I can finally put a face to the name," she noted, as she shook my hand. "Thank you," I said. "Nice to meet you." As we departed, she stopped and asked. Have you applied for any other positions here? I told her I had just applied for the trainer position earlier that week. She responded, "Oh I think you'd be great. Hope you get it." On my way back to my desk I stopped by my supervisor's office. I asked did he know who Natalie Wolfe, and he told me she was the CFO. Three weeks later I was the new trainer in the call center. Fate called on that Wednesday, and I did not just hear her. I listened.

So…

What are you like half mother goose? Cool story.

Cool Story?

*Yes, you are the definition of a "Cool Story."
You're two for two right now, but they might as
well be made up. They served you no purpose.
They are just stories, simply stories! I do not
understand. You should be able to answer why
you breathe and why you hear, easily with what
you have just told me. You have these life
experiences to learn and draw from, yet they are
nothing but camp side, chicken noodle soup
stories. The answers you need, you have already
lived. You just need to check your work.*

Well, I know working at the nursing home made
me a much better grandson. My grandmother was
in a hospital nursing rehab facility recovering from
a bad fall. My mom and aunts had rotational visits
throughout the week, but there were occasions in
which no one could make it. Between the 3 aunts,
there were four grandkids, and I was the closest, so
naturally the first ask was for me. In the past,
before I ever worked at the nursing home, I would
have passed the responsibility every chance I
could. Working in that nursing home opened my

eyes, and there was no way I could close them on my grandmother. I walked into her room at the right time. She was having a nightmare. She had rolled over and sandwiched herself between the wall and the mattress. She was yelling, "Help, help! God, please help me!" I rushed over and gently woke her up, thankful to be there. I was only supposed to be there from 9am to 12pm. My aunt was coming in at noon. I ended up staying until she fell asleep that night. We talked about everything from murder to marriage. Without the experience of working in a nursing home, I would not have known how important it is to spend as much time with your love ones at place like this. It was the most enjoyable time I spent with my grandmother since I was born.

Thanks, another cool story, but so what? So, what YOU had a great time with your grandmother? So, what YOU got a job promotion? Bla bla bla..

What do you mean, so what? Bla bla bla?

So, what about you? Who cares about you?

YOU DO! YOU CARE! DIDN'T YOU ASK, WHY DO I SMELL? WHY DO I HEAR? I'VE

NEVER THOUGHT ABOUT THAT IN MY
LIFE!

*THAT'S OBVIOUS! SOUNDS TO ME LIKE
YOU'VE JUST BEEN OUT HERE DOING YOU,
AND LOOK WHERE YOU GOT YOU.*

Look?! Look, where? I can't see. Remember? But
I will tell you what it looks like to a blind man. It
looks like I am stuck with a blind guide dog asking
me questions that are leading me nowhere.

*No. You were in 'nowhere' before I met you. I
showed up to help you get from nowhere to
somewhere. I can leave you with 'nobody' in this
nowhere or you can get out of your feelings and
see and smell what is going on.*

If you really want to help just tell me what you're
talking about. Seriously. It would be much quicker.
I have been hearing all my life and not once did
hearing ever tell me why I am alive. I see no point
in any of this. Yeah, working at the Call Center
made me a better listener and speaker. Helped me
learn how to get the point and not waste people's
time. Whoopi! Hopefully, you can take something
from my story and stop wasting mine!

Wasting your time? You have no time! Time is for the free and you are stuck. There is nothing you could possibly be doing because you do not have any other option. I am not here to waste your time, but to show you where your time is. You are so worried about you. Accept that you are stuck and that its bigger than you and your feelings.

How can you show me how to use my time, if you just said I don't have any?

By guiding you. As I said before, I can be your guide if you like, but if you would like to go it alone, I can guide you to that path as well. It's up to you, my friend.

Friend? Let us just stick with guide. My friends would understand where I am coming from.

A real friend knows it does not matter where you came from, it matters where you are going, and you need a guide for that.

Guide me where? I let you guide me, and my hearing comes back? Just so I can hear water. Then you guide me to my sense of smell. Smelling underwater? Sounds like drowning to me. Who wants to smell river water anyway? Why would that be rewarding? You think I'm a fish?

*You know what, yes. Yes, why not? You are a fish!
Your attitude stinks of fish, so you must be.*

What are you talking about? Where are you taking
me?

You are a fish, a bottom feeding fish.

Wait, I don't want to go deeper. I can feel the
pressure in my head. It is too much!

Next stop, the riverbed!

Take me back up!

*But this is where you wanted to be. You wanted to
be a bottom dweller. Your conversation said it all.
I do not want to hear it now. Ha, hear. Funny I
have the option to hear because I know why I can.
I am the guide, the guide who knows the way to
your answer. Smelling and hearing, those two
small rewards you care nothing about, are steps to
an answer you may never solve because neither of
which you still know why you were given the
ability to do. Since I am not your grandmother,
who I wonder if, really enjoyed your company as
much you hers, I will get efficiently and straight to
the point as the valuable lesson you learned
listening in the Call Center, guide you undividedly
to what you want- the bottom, to dwell in your*

feelings. That pressure you feel in your ears is the weight of your self-inflicted sorrows. You would rather carry them yourself anchoring you to the bottom as you drag and mope for still being alive. You do not need me for that. Enjoy your journey my senseless friend.

Bottom Dwelling

I could not move. The pressure was too heavy. I tried to push up off the river bottom but was not strong enough. It felt like a giant's foot was on my back. I tried continuously to push up, straining for a hulk like strength, but to no avail. I was stuck belly flat only able to turn my head from cheek to cheek. As I lay there, stuck, my mind wandered. I have heard of left for dead, but never left for alive. I could not figure it out. Part of me was happy to finally be left alone, not having to hear this unknown guide directing me to life, or death. Who knows what his intentions were? All I knew was that I missed my father. As I lay there cemented to the floor, I let my body surrender to the pressure, as my mind searched for peace. All I could think was, "I MISS MY DAD." I repeated it over and over. I miss my dad, I miss my dad, I miss my dad. Maybe out of disbelief, but also comfort the acknowledgment kept him present, kept him fresh, kept the pain fresh, which I was afraid to let go. I did not want to not miss my dad, and his death was the last, most present moment I had of him. That pain I felt was the void he had always filled, and I needed it. In all my years I had never said aloud, or even had the thought that I miss my dad. My mother got all my misses. Dad was dad, until now. Now Dad was missed, and at this moment I was physically, exactly where I was mentally. I was stuck, and perhaps submitting to being stuck. All I could think about was that I missed him. I was in my feelings because that is where my dad was. I felt to get out of my feelings would be leaving him, and I had never been without my dad.

Since the passing of my father, I had dreamed more about my father than I ever had, and in each dream, he was still alive. I knew he was not alive, but in my dreams he was. I lost all reason and accepted this pseudo reality. I would cry heavily and hug him with all my might every time he showed up in my dreams. It was as if my mind was giving me endorphin filled dreams to numb the shock of reality. The night before my fall, when I had finally finished preparing and getting my clothes together for the funeral, I tried to sleep, but the endorphin drip had been pulled. It left me restless and unable to get comfortable. I awoke early from a dream of my father in the coffin, dead. I can normally control my dreams, or at the least influence them, but every time I dreamed about my dad it was so real, I couldn't notice until I woke up. I woke up knowing I was about to do exactly what I had just dreamed. It felt like I was having déjà vu before the "vu." I asked myself, how could I dream that already? Especially because I was still missing my dad, not "Dad you will be missed." There is a difference. "I miss my dad" allows me to be just as present with my dad as the day he passed, stagnant in my thoughts. "Dad you will be missed" is triumphant. It is overcoming. The dream of my father in the coffin felt like a "Dad you will be missed" dream. Why would I want that? Why would I want to move my dad to a past tense? Death is already the greatness physical distance; I could not let him die in my mind. Since I can control that, that is where he remained- in mind. If being stuck down to the river bottom due to my feelings allows me to be present with my dad, then home sweet home it is. "Isn't that right, dad?" I asked myself. I miss you man. I really miss you. I do not know what that guide was trying to do, but he should have taken me to the bottom from the start. He could have kept all those 'why do you smell… why do you hear' questions for someone else. He should have let me be right here with you.

> "I bet his next question was going to be why
> do you taste?

Why do I taste?

I taste so I know what I like to eat.

Ok, tell me about your most memorable taste.

How about first? You tell me how I am still breathing underwater!

I am not the one that is stuck…

Yeah, yeah, yeah, I know. What is my strongest memory of taste?"

Well, I don't remember when I first paid attention to having the ability to taste, but I do remember my dad's sandwiches, and since we are here because of my dad, it is fitting that I speak about it. They always tasted better than mine. His sandwiches never failed to satisfy my taste buds. Maybe it was the whole Law of Diminishing Returns tricking me because I never got his sandwiches repeatedly. They were spread out amongst eating school food and mom letting me practice indecency by making my own lunch while she supervised, but nonetheless that one occasional sandwich from him was a memorable footlong meal to me every time. I remember watching him make the sandwich, trying to remember everything I saw for future duplication. When I finally had a chance to repeat his creation of palate perfection, I never could match the taste, quality, and satisfaction of what my dad had made. My sandwich was always unbalanced. Never equally satisfying my hunger and my taste buds the way one bite of my father's sandwich would. I created a "settlers' sandwich." It is not the best, but you will settle for it.

I remember a Sunday after church, we had decided to go to this restaurant called O'Charley's. We had recently fallen in love with their complimentary yeast rolls. Dad, Mom, my sister Brittany, we all loved them. As for entrees, mom knew she was getting Brittany the kids' meal, so the big question was what I wanted. I saw prime rib on the menu, and all I could think about were some delicious barbeque ribs. I said, "I want the prime ribs." My dad said, "That's a steak, you want a steak?" Childishly confused and slightly embarrassed that I did not know prime rib was a steak and wanting to hide my ignorance, I said yes. Like any good parent, he knew I did not know prime rib was a steak. I know my dad knew based off what he ordered. He told mom, "Go head and let that boy get the steak," as he proceeded to order the club sandwich. That was not a normal Sunday dinner type meal for him, but he knew what he was doing. Sure enough, the food comes out, and I see my greyish brown prime rib with a sliver of fat to go with it. In my wildest 10-year-old imagination, I was not expecting the prime rib to look like this. Still holding on to my boyish pride, my dad asked whether I needed some help cutting it, and I said no as I wildly zig-zagged through the steak with my knife like a child learning to color within the lines. I finally was able to saw off a piece of steak. My cutting skills were so bad it looked like it was gnawed off. The taste was less satisfying than my "settlers' sandwich." My naivety still had me believing it was going to taste something like ribs, just without the barbeque sauce. Dad saw my face after the first bite, but still let me sit there for a while before he said, "Lets trade," which I gladly did. I recognized ham, turkey, bacon, and bread any day of the week. What I was not expecting was that it would taste as good as a bite of one of his homemade sandwiches. How? I thought his sandwiches were the best I had ever had, but now this. It was not until I was much older and had experienced some things that help me realize why his sandwich always tasted better than mine. Dad, you made it with love. You may have ordered an O'Charleys sandwich, but you doctored it with love before you gave it to me. It is like when my sister worked at a McDonalds, she served a lot hamburgers and fries, but the hamburgers and fries she brought home were far different from the ones she served. Through the drive thru window, she chored out whatever the customer wanted, but the food that came home had love on it. That was my missing ingredient. You made your sandwich like you were making it for someone you love. I made my sandwich like it was a chore, and it tasted like it. I always did my chores just well enough that you and mom would settle for it. It was not until I got older and made some omelets for a girl I was interested in when it hit me. She absolutely went crazy over them, and honestly, she was not the type of girl to go crazy over anything I did. She told her mom, grandma, and sisters how great they were. Funny thing is I knew they were awesome, humbly speaking, because I love omelets and I love making them, and I thought I loved her. When I made them, I made them with love. When I gave them, I gave them with love. Love is the MVP seasoning for your taste buds. I learned that day the secret to your sandwiches. No matter what you are making to eat, whether for you or someone else, if it does not have love in it, the best it could be is food someone would settle for.

I thought I learned that day about seasoning with love, but I did not comprehend the lesson. I had not grasped the communicative gift in love's seasoning. They say it is no such thing as mistakes, only lessons learned. Among all the sadness and pain of my dad being gone, I also fade in an out of a mistake I made. I play back as much of my father as I can. Rewinding all the way back to the beginning of my memories until now, but never far away is the memory of the last time you asked him to get you something to eat. It was the Sunday before he passed. I know you did not personally ask me to get you something to eat, the stroke had left you very limited in communication, but through your actions he let Brittany know he did not want any more hospital food. I got a text from your sister, asking me to pick you something up to eat before I came back to the hospital. I got out of Church around 12:15pm and I had a meeting setup at 1pm. This meeting could have been postponed. I was the reason for the meeting, but I thought I could make it quick. I did not want to go to the hospital, drop off the food then leave, so I went to the meeting. I am in the meeting mad at myself because I should not be there; I should be "about my father's business." It is well into 2 o'clock and Brittany calls. "Where are you?" It was not an irritated tone but a very 'get your butt over here with dad's food' tone. I closed the meeting after getting off the phone. They had already sent me the type of food you wanted, so I headed to restaurant to pick it up. I get to the restaurant in the heart of Sunday dinner traffic. I am looking at my watch with each slow ordering customer, with all the stress and tensioned forehead of a road raged drive. I finally make it to the front of the line to order, only to find out they ran out of sweet potatoes. Had I gotten there when I was supposed to, this would not have been a problem. I storm out of there with nobody to be mad at but myself and head over to a restaurant I know has everything he wanted. I walked in expecting to see large after-church crowd, but that was not the case. I walk right up to the ordering desk, but there is no one there. I see the people in the kitchen cooking, but no one is coming to the desk to take my order. Any other time I would have patiently waited, but trying to make up time for my mistake, I go to the hostess and have her go get somebody to take my order. A manager comes out, apologizes, and takes my order. I assumed with the lack of crowd I would get your food quickly. The only quick thing in the restaurant was my realization of why nobody was in here. The service was awful. Due to my decision-making, my dad's food which was texted to me around 12:15pm did not get to you until 3:30pm. No matter how hurriedly I tried to make up the time I had loss during my flawed choices, it was nothing I could do now. I ran out of the car, ran to the elevator, frantically hit the button, impatiently waited as the elevator stopped on floors that were not important to my destination, sped walk to your door, only to deliver your food and see your face. I watched your eyes as Brittany/my sister pulled your food out of the bag. She opened your food up and placed on your tray and wheeled it over to him. You just looked at it and shook your head. Brittany asked whether you wanted it. You shook your head again and said no and tilted your head back into the pillow.

I think he was disappointed, and he should have been. Maybe it had nothing to do with me, but he had every right to be disinterested in that food. From the moment I got that text, I had no intentions of seasoning his food with love. His food seasoned with love would have arrived hours ago. Whether he was hungry or not, whether he was sick of the hospital food, or the company in the room I believe he would've have taken a bite. He would have reciprocated the same love he showed me the day I bought him lunch from this stuffed spud place I had been telling him about. They had onions on the spud, and he did not want onions, but he ate it anyway because it was seasoned with the effort of love. The season of love satisfies all taste buds and covers dislikes.

Dad if your listening, I said all that to say I am sorry I did not serve your last meal from me with the love you with which you have always seasoned mine. With the thankfulness of hindsight and the regrets of present thoughts, I live with this lesson. Season your food with love.

Finnick

Hey, hey! You still down there?

Who said that?

Man, you have been rambling for a while now. Are you ok?

You heard me?

How could I not? Your vibrations were everywhere.

Why didn't you say anything?

I did not want to interrupt.

Interrupt?

Yea, you seemed to be in deep conversation, too. I kept coming back around for curiosity sake.

Curiosity? More like nosey.

Well, if nosey suits you, but I will stick with curious. I would have spoken sooner, but you

*never interrupt a man talking to himself. Had to
wait for one of you to leave.*

You must think I am crazy?

*I don't know what you are, and that is why I kept
circling back.*

You can say it. You think I am crazy! I don't know
what is crazier, talking to myself or still being
alive, stuck to the bottom of a river talking to
mystery guest number 2.

*My apologies. I am no mystery. I am Finnick, but
you can call me Fin. What do you mean stuck? You
may really be crazy, but all you got to do is get up.*

I have tried that. It is not that simple. I can barely
lift my head up. It feels like there's a giant's foot
on my back.

I bet that giant's foot is your dad.

What?

*I heard you talking about your missing your dad
each time I came by.*

Like I said nosey!

Like I said concerned.

I thought it was curious.

*Or, curious. It was a C word, and both of those
work. Anyway, my guess is that weight you feel
that is keeping you stuck is all your fault.*

My fault? I did not ask to be here! I did not ask for
my dad to be dead. I did not ask to miss him! I did
not ask for any of this!

*Do you hear yourself? I did not do this. I did not
do that. If you did not ask for any of it, why are
you in possession of it? If I do not want something,
I am not going to take it. That's like overeating; If
I just kept eating and eating even when I did not
want it, eventually I would be like you, stuck. The
only difference is you're stuck in your feelings.*

My feelings? Here you go. You sound like
someone I recently met.

*Well, they were not lying. Get out of your feelings!
How long do plan for this pity party to last?*

You ever lost somebody close to you?

*Yes sir. If you live long enough that is a certainty,
or short enough in my case. You are not the
founder of loss. I recently loss both my brothers.*

Well, what did you do?

*In the words of my mom, I KEPT IT MOVING!
Keep it moving was my mom's favorite phrase, so
that is what I have done. I have been moving since
she passed. All those feelings that you wear like a
favorite outfit, I left. I felt that wave coming, that
emotional wave of nakedness and lack of direction
from the void of my mother. Before the paralysis of
it all could make a home in me, I took that one
memory of my mom saying keep it moving. That
memory is why I am not you. I kept it moving!
Anytime I feel that wave of feelings getting closer I
move faster. If those feelings ever caught up with
me, they would not just weigh me down. They
would crush me.*

So, you just ran?

No, I did not run. I moved. Running implies I am scared. I am not scared. I moved, to not be stuck. My body was losing the want to. I felt myself pruning, shrinking. When I began to move, I stretched back out and exhaled that tightness off my chest, stopping myself from shrinking. I have not stopped moving since. I know the day I stop moving is the day I start to atrophy from the grip of emotions I have been avoiding. I purposely keep moving, always occupying my mental space. Not giving my mind any time to reminisce. Instead, I fill my mind with the next destination. The day I let my body rest is the day the battle of the yin of my body starts to lose ground to the yang of my mind. We are no different. Our yin and yang operate the same way. Every day our yin and yang wrestle for leverage trying to gain control of how we will live. My physical "yin" can't let my mental "yang" be the majority shareholder, so I keep my yang at a deficit. If not, I would be in your situation. Your yang is in full control. It has shrunk your yin. Your body's purpose has dehydrated as you physically have drawn in, leaving you unable to move. You're mentally bloated as your "yang" has taken over your body's energy. Your body is addictively feeding on all your pain and sadness...

That weight of a giant's foot you feel on your back is your Yang. I never fed my Yang. Once I realized keeping moving shrank it, I never stopped moving. I accept the fact that I must keep moving to starve my Yang. Any time I feel a little shift of my Yin over my Yang, I move faster. The lighter I am, the freer I move. Looking at you, I have no regrets on my decision.

You would rather park in your pity and idle your life away. Like blood rushing to a bruise, you are sending all your energy to you, but you cannot feel your void with you without pulling away from another part of you. That is a never-ending cycle pouring pain on top of sadness on top loneliness until you clot. Stopping everything from flowing the way it should. That clot will continue to grow if you feed it. It knows no satisfaction. But it will deplete you. Therefore, you cannot move. Your body is too busy tending to your abyss of feelings. You must get out of them because your feelings do not care about you. You care about them. Your feelings are selfish and greedy. They affect your body the way cold weather affects it. Your ear gets cold, so it starts pulling from the furthest parts of you. Your fingers, nose, toes, ears, heart all know if the heart goes, who cares about your extremities.

The problem is that this is not a matter of the heart, this is a matter of the smarts. You must get out of your heart and start thinking. I outsmarted my feelings, and they know everything about me. Yet, they still have not found me. If I could pat my own self on the back, I would. Maybe when I help you up you can pat my back for me.

Help? You think "running" is going to help me?

Not run, move.

I do not want to run or move. I do not want to leave the memories of my dad. Those memories keep him alive.

Thinking like that is going to keep you stuck as well. Do not worry about leaving your memories. You cannot. They belong to you and will come for you if you stay still long enough. Instead, keep moving and creating new memories. The memories that started me on my journey must fight upriver like salmon through the crowd of new memories to get to me. If I ever decide to relive those old thoughts, I *will just stay still and let them stampede me until I am trampled to the bottom of the river like you. Right?*

Well, when you put it like that, it sounds like I made a bad decision.

Your right! It is. You could be out here living! Doing what you really want to do. Instead of letting dead weight anchor you down. All you got to do is start thinking of where you would want to be if nothing had ever happened. Find that place and create from there. That dead weight will start lighting up immediately.

If my father never died? I do not know where I would be, but I would not be here.

There you go! Keep it up! Keep it light. What would you be doing right now?

"Keep it light. Keep it light."

Now try to move a little.

Hey! I can lift my head.

Exactly! Misery loves company, and you are finally telling the company you are leaving! Cut the lights on. The pity party is over!

I am standing!

Of course, your load has lightened. Now most important try to step. You are going to have to move because it will not be long before they return. You are not strong enough yet to fight and move, but if you follow me, I will show you how to always stay ahead of them.

How is that?

By not turning. I am living on the line. Linear living. I keep straight, no turns. When you turn you always run into something you left behind. Memories run on constant loops. They keep circling back. Showing up to remind you then leave you with your feelings again. That is where situations like yours start. Some people will not move because they like what the memories remind them of. It is not until that memory fades off on to the loop again that emotion fades, and you sink back into your feelings waiting for another loop to temporarily numb you from the emptiness. An addict of misery, getting high off your pity, it is quite selfish to be so caught up in your feelings you stop living. Especially when you could be charting

*new waters and new memories every day. So,
what do you say?*

I hear you and your persuasive lifestyle.

But…

But selfish, aren't you selfish? What is the
difference between your selfishness and mine?

Explain.

Well aren't you so into yourself that you close
yourself off from your own self? You're constantly
on the move, dodging your feelings when all your
feelings want to do is come home. The avoidance
of feelings may allow your numbness, but you are
not living. You are just surviving. You did not
check on me because of the way you felt for me.
You left that feeling behind. You stopped for you.
I am just another experience you can fill your mind
up with as you keep moving.

*Regardless of why I stopped to check on you, I did.
How do you know if I had my feelings, I would
have stopped? I likely would have kept going,
maybe not even traveled this way.*

Maybe, but like you said, feelings move on loops. You likely would have turned around because that is what feelings do. They weigh on you.

Turn around for what? So, I can end up like you? Weighed down? Stuck? Waiting to die. I might not be living but surviving is much better than where you are standing. There are two choices- fight or flight. But you chose neither. You chose not to choose, and you think that makes you better than me. You are so into your feelings and the brief euphoria of pain and pleasure mix of memories of your father, that you would rather stay there. You pulled up a chair to the buffet of your feelings and have eaten so much you cannot get out. I do not know if you could get up, you would want to. You are the junky who never leaves the dope house. You would rather shoot up, shoot up, and shoot up than to make a sober decision toward fight or flight. You are the definition of a junky. I do not even know if selfish is the right word for you. If I had feelings, maybe I could say I have sympathy for you.

Well I have feelings and I feel nothing for you.

Of course you don't. All your feelings are for yourself. They are not even for your dad. They are of your dad, but you do not feel for him. You feel for yourself. It is you weighing you down. All you must do is make a choice.

You said I did choose. I chose not to choose. Which means there are three choices, not two, right?

There are two choices in LIFE. You made the choice of death. To not do anything is to die. You are stuck to the bottom of a riverbed. Remember? Just now able to stand. I do not know how you're still alive, but death is in this water my friend.

Friend? You're no friend of mine.

Friend, right now you need any friend willing to be a friend.

Friends have feelings. You have motives.

Whatever my motive could possibly be, you are going to die either way. Stuck or moving, it's coming. I just heard you talking and figured you might as well occupy my mind and talk to me.

Exactly- you did not stop to help me; you stop to help yourself. Selfish!

I never denied I was not, but I offered my way of life as an example of what you could be doing. You could follow my lead until you figure out where you are going. That is much better than where you stand, literally.

When you are stuck everything sounds good. The excitement of finally being able to move compounded with the fact I have no senses has dampened my perception of your honesty so anything but where I stand is appealing. I mean maybe you're right. What is the worst that could happen?

Alright, all you must do is go to a place when your dad was still alive. A time when the thought of death was far from your mind. Do not go to a specific memory, just a time. We are trying to lighten you up. You must lose these weighted feelings you are carrying.

I think it is working. I am wiggling my toes.

Good, now for the tough part. Let us go back to when everything started, when you first found out he was at the hospital.

Yeah, I remember walking into his room at the ER. He looked disappointed like he had let me down. I wonder if that is the look all fathers share at that moment, but he said he felt alright and the doctors said it was just some high blood pressure and diet issues.

Good, good. Now take that ball it up and look for a door in your mind labeled "It never happened." Once you find it, toss it in there.

What?

Yes, you got to do it. It seems fictitious to do something like this, but your mind can do some incredible things, especially when it comes to pain. It is better to grab those first memories of your dad being sick and throw them out.

I don't know. I do not know if I want to put these memories away. This is like starting a book and stopping three quarters of the way through.

Exactly! If there is no ending, did it happen? It is like a dream that you forget as soon as you wake up. There are temporary traces as you come out of the fog of sleep, but by the time you get to moving around it is gone. It is like releasing an air bubble in water. You watch for a novelty minute then move on only to look up and see its gone.

Yeah, but my father's ending is not my father's ending. It is my ending to my father's story. To remove these memories would do worse than good. If memories run on a loop, and I destroy the bridge to get back around, then what? There will always be a gap. Have you ever met someone with a gap?

I taught middle school fresh out of college. I had a student whose mother was addicted to drugs while he was in the womb. He was a great kid. I say great because he made no excuses to not try. We were working on multiplication. He could not do it. He could not remember. His mother doing drugs while carrying him affected his memorization. I could write on a piece of paper 2 x 2 =4. Then erase the 4 but not so well that you could not make out the 4 if you really wanted to. I would ask again what is 2 x 2? He looked at me, looked at his paper, looked back at me, and started to cry. He cried real genuine tears. I could see in his eyes confusion because he was trying but could not find it. He was hurt he could not remember. That bubble of air had floated on him and no matter how hard he searched his brain for the answer, it was gone. I do not want to look for a memory of my father and only get a vanishing glimpse of confusion. I want to always be able to recall his story, our story, and my story of him. You are right to compare life to a dream living your way. There is a part of your story you cannot remember, but you opted to forget. Maybe I was mistaken to say you run, but you were also mistaken to say you move. You do not move. You wander like a dementia patient. I bet you have those detached, filmy, glazed over, nursing home eyes as you float in and out of acts in the play of life. A play in which you have opted to be an extra. A temporary role with no beginning or an end. Lost, appearing, and disappearing before you get attached. You are a dream to the strangers you meet. You had me sold on the rewards of this dream life, but the fine print of living this kind of life does not match. The pleasures of living a dream are unmatched, but the inability to hold on to them is the curse that causes you to continue wandering, chasing that next one, only for it to slip through the fingers of your mind because you wanted to forget the memories that bridge all your experiences together. You ever wonder why you always remember your nightmares? I think it is the reality holding you down, not letting you up until you are ready. It's why you always wake up too early from a dream and try to rush back to sleep only to never catch that dream again. But a nightmare, you can wake from it thinking you beat it only to fall right back into it. Dreams are the fairytales of life that if you are not careful you can get lost in them. The reality wakes us up before we can hold on to these grandiose dreams and become satisfied. No one would ever wake from a dream on purpose. Dreams are better than life. That is why every time we wake up from a dream, it is always too soon. Reality knows whether we would ever reach the end of a dream, but nightmares, that is where reality wants us- facing our truths. There are breakthroughs for life in nightmares that our dreams never uncover. You are trying to live a dream, afraid to face the truth of your nightmare. When I was younger, no matter what I may have been thinking about before falling asleep, I would have a very specific nightmare. A nightmare where this man-monster called Freddy

Krueger would start chasing me. He was a horror film cult like monster when I was a child. My nightmares of him were relentlessly consistent. I had never seen any of the Freddy Krueger movies. My childlike imagination could not have handled that, but I had caught glimpses of the commercials for his movies. All I knew was that he came while you slept. I do not know how he work himself into my imagination, but once he was there, he was there. I tried everything to stop myself from thinking about him, but it never worked. He would just show up and start chasing me. I would run but could never run as fast as I felt like I should be running. I would fight and fight trying to wake up but never could. It was always right when I had finally given up trying force my self-awake that somehow, I would wake up. After a couple of adolescent years of Freddy Krueger terrorizing my sleep as I tried to force myself awake, I made a breakthrough. I always ran each time he showed up, but disappointingly I was never fast enough to change the narrative of the nightmare. This time however, he had chased me into an apartment building. I was running down a hallway and it was a wall there. Scared out of mind, survival mode on high, and a blend of cartoonish superpowers I told myself run through the wall. I ran through it. As walls came up, I was able to speed up and bust through them. I had broken through my speed problem by breaking through walls. Feeling I had a little bit of creative breathing room I ask myself why not fly. If I fly, I can get away from him for good. I started running faster and faster and then jumped into the air. Next thing I know, I was flying. I was soaring through the air. From that point on, every time he showed up, I did not try to force myself awake. I ran as fast as I ever have, jumped in the air, and flew. Freddy Krueger started appearing less and less until not at all.

See you kept it moving! That is what I have been saying.

No, me running like you would have been me avoiding sleep or me trying to sleep in my parents' room, or any place where I could hide my vulnerability. I was too young to think about not going to sleep, and too old to be trying to sleep in my parents' room, so I had face it. Whenever he showed up, I was going to have to deal with it, and the truth is that if every time Freddy showed up, I woke up. I would be like you. Afraid to sleep. Not being able to wake out of my nightmare made me. I do not know I can fly if I do not face it, and me being able to fly turned my nightmare into a dream. You will keep having the same nightmare until you end it, and the ending of a nightmare is a dream. Maybe my father's death is my new nightmare. If so, I'd rather keep having this nightmare until it becomes my dream, than to make my father's existence a dream.

So are you coming or not?

You weren't listening?

For the most part, I heard what you were saying. I was moving around while you were talking. You know I do not have the ability to stay in one place. Are you coming?

No, I got to figure this out and see it to the end.

The end? We just getting started. I got it figured it out for you just, pick your foot up and let us go!

How about you just go?

You're still here?!

Who are you? You know him?

Remember I told you. You were mystery guest number two. Meet number one. I kind of know him. I know him more than a stranger but less than a friend. He was supposed to be my guide out of here.

No at all. Had I known you were with him I would not have slowed down. I should have known he was close by.

You know him, too?

We have crossed paths before. Sadly, he is still the same as I remember him. Moving around the same way as always.

If you know me so well then you should be thanking me.

Thanking you? This water must be getting to you.

Yes! You most definitely should be thanking me. I could of...

You could have done nothing! Everything you did, I allowed.

Oh, is that right the great puppet master orchestrating behind the scenes. Well, my strings have been cut for a while now. You allow nothing of me I do not allow of myself.

Your nose must still be growing because we both know that is a lie! Even without strings, you do not punctuate one sentence of your life without permission. You did exactly what I wanted you to do.

What is that?

Fail!

And you think he will not? Look at him, had I had more time he would have been mine. Just know if I see him again, I will not be his friend.

Friend? You're only familiar with the word not the definition. Now leave!

Still Here?

So, you have been here the whole time? I thought you had left me for dead.

I have been close by, but I did not leave you for dead. I left you for your feelings.

You left me with my feelings and Fin, Mr. Puppet Master.

Yes, I did, but that was necessary.

I heard you say that you allowed him.

Yes, I was listening the entire time, and I could have interrupted but I wanted him to offer you anther current. Upstream or downstream? It was your choice though.

Which stream did he offer?

What do you think?

Downstream. He seemed to be going with the flow not looking for any resistance, just cruising.

Ok.

Ok. What? Am I right that he was offering downstream, or are you upstream?

Up or down depends on who you are. We are all different. Some would find it hard to go with the flow and cruise. They would consider that upstream, but I was not leading you upstream. In your case, it does not matter whether you flow up or down stream because you do not belong in a stream.

So, if neither current specifically is good for me, what are you doing? Why did you run him off? At least he tried to help me. Why are you still here with me if you are not leading me in any direction but 'stuck.'

Because you are lost and before you pick a direction you have to know where you are. Then you can find your way. But before you can find your way, you have to fix your compass. Your magnets to life have been drowned out from your pity party of feelings. For you, either up or down stream does not matter, you are still drowning. You need to get out. Your compass will let you know when to go with the flow and when to fight against the current.

Well, how do I get my compass back?

You should already know what I am going to say. Your answers will show you the way.

You mean to those questions? Why do I smell? why do I hear? Why do I etcetera, etcetera?

Exactly. Why can you do those things?

I got a why question for you. Why don't you go first?

Aww, how polite of you, but no thank you. Your why of me will be answered by the why of yourself.

Well could you at least...

Guide you? Of course. Since you are being so polite, how about you tell me what it means?

Really?

Yes. this is an easy one.

I guess, to put somebody else in front of you, to look out for another person.

Good, so take that and combine that with why you smell? Mix politeness with the ability to smell and think about the story you told me of when you worked at the nursing home. How did you use your smell?

Are you saying I used my smell for others?

Yes, in a way.

So, you are telling me the reason I can smell, breathe, whatever is for other people?

Precisely. If you went on that floor and only used your smell for you, you would have walked past all those patients, done what you had to do, and left quicker than you entered. But that smell triggered you to think about someone else. It happened to be those patients who could not escape what you could. How polite.

I was just doing what I would want somebody to do for me.

Hence the word polite. Now take three deep breaths through you nose and tell me if you can smell anything?

Hey, I do! I can smell the water and a strange fishiness.

Alright, good! Now what about hearing?

I hear for the same reasons. I hear for others.

Explain.

When I was listening to that lady complain about her bill and her husband being in the hospital, once I realized she was not paying, I could have terminated the call, but I listened. I listened when she said she was going to kill herself, and I heard it. My body heard that, and I went into autopilot. It felt like someone was working in me; it was my voice talking, I recognized that, but what I was saying was not premeditated. It just flowed.

Because it was genuine. Politeness is deeper than habits of
niceness. Those are just manners. You do it long enough and it sticks is not what politeness is. Politeness is instinctive. Your smell, your hearing, and yes, your taste was given to you to be used politely.

Taste?

Yep, even your taste. What did you say about your father making sandwiches?

He made them with love.

Love- and what does that taste like?

Tastes like someone who made it like they would want it to be made. Made like they knew your taste buds better than you.

Hmm, sounds polite.

Sounds! Sounds! You probably already know, but I can hear! And my taste is back, too. Yuck! Why is it so salty? I think I am good on the taste part right now. gross!

Ha, ha, ha.

Well, what is next? Let's go!

Go where exactly?

I do not know. I thought you were telling me.

No, I am just helping you gather your belongings. You are still missing a couple of them?

I am still missing a couple things. I can only hear, taste, and smell.

Tell me about touch. Tell me about a time when touch answered the question of why you can.

I know exactly when I realized the importance of touch. It was an unexpected and unknowingly needed, eye-opening experience that validated a medical story I had read about the consequences of babies going untouched. There was a study done that babies who were not touched, held, hugged, or loved on enough could stop growing, and if the situation lasted long enough, even die. I do not

123

know why I remembered this random bit of "did you know, knowledge." I had no kids, nor was I around babies enough to be concerned about this. It was mostly out of bewilderment and future practicality that I tucked this nugget of information away for a rainy day. My rainy day came when I moved to Minneapolis. I had lived in Nashville my entire life, from preschool to college. I had been working in the same city for 8 years when I decided to move to Minneapolis for post grad work. During my introduction to the city, I never knew the whole time I had been walking in the rain. I knew nobody in Minneapolis, the closest people I knew were 8 hours away in Chicago. I had moved up almost 2 months before school started and was staying in an extended stay hotel. I had a checklist of items to accomplish and figured it would be easier to do them from Minneapolis than back home. I needed to find an apartment, complete school registration, interview for a couple of jobs, and become acclimated with the city. The biggest part for me was the acclimation of the city, and the key to my acclimation was finding a church. If everything in this city had the potential to be different from what I had known, the one line in the sand could be the Church. The commonality of worship could bring a since of comforted familiarity that I found myself wanting and needing in my new environment. An environment that would be changing soon, it was warm now, but the fall was approaching. All I heard was how cold it is in Minnesota and how it can snow at any time. Thankfully, in pursuit of accomplishing all my checklist items, a few fell into my lap surprisingly quickly. I had a close friend in Nashville whose aunt lived in Minneapolis. She connected me with two mindless jobs that I did not even have to interview for. They both fit perfectly around my college schedule. I filled out everything that they needed online and knocked out two birds with one stone. I would not start either one of them until around the time school started, so I spent my days calling apartments, checking for vacancies. I used my apartment searching to find a place to live and to help acclimate with the city. Based off the area of the apartment, I would determine whether to follow up with the leasing offices. The first couple of days living in the extended stay hotel were good. I was making progress on my checklist, and I was excited to be on new adventure-my first true adventure. It was not until my fourth day in the hotel and not having any luck with vacancies in the apartments, shopping at the gas station and eating

McDonalds every day that I woke up that afternoon disoriented. I looked around and could see the light sneaking past the black-out curtains in the room. I sat up trying to figure out where I was. I had never felt this before and did not know how to react to it. I was discombobulated. I did not know what to tell my brain to tell my body how to feel. It all just blended into, "Where am I?" Growing up, hotels were the embodiment of fun- jumping on the beds, indoor pools, staying up late, and waking up to your family. As an adult, I still shared that same enjoyment for hotels, enjoying king size beds, not making it them up, room service, and going out in the city. All of that was great, but living in the hotel in a city you do not yet know was mysterious. There had not been a time in my life where being in hotel was not surrounded by a certainty of fun and familiarity, but now I was waking up absent of any experiences I could use for reference. Hotels, I once thought of as one room mansions having everything I wanted, now were showing with each day that they were absent of what I needed. As the fog of disillusion cleared, I came back to my senses. The initial anxiety had left me frozen in the bed as I peppered myself with questions like a moody superstar after a bad game at a postgame press conference.

"How long until I found an apartment? Next question. How long will you be living in this hotel? Next question. What if you have to go back home? Next question. What if you do not find an apartment you can afford? Next question. Did you move too fast? Next question. Are you being too picky? Umm, any more questions not centered around my move? No, alright, thank you for your time."

I got up and looked out my window to make sure nobody had gotten into my car packed with 70% of everything I owned. Still lacking familiarity with my surroundings and not in the mood for discovery, the golden arches of McDonald's once again were shining like a lighthouse of comfort foods in a new place. I had eaten McDonald's for lunch or dinner every day since being in Minneapolis. One, it was the closest food place to the hotel, and two, it felt like home. McDonald's are everywhere! McDonald's and satellite radio gave me an expected "everything is going to be alright" feeling. Eating McDonald's in the hotel parking lot and listening to the stations I listened to back home were the natural Zoloft supplement I needed to give me a calmness. I listened to the same stations I listened to back home, so in my car it felt like I had never left home. The hotel did not, the people living in the hotel did not, not even the staff felt like home. It was not that I was homesick. It was that I did not have a home. I was trying to make a home in transition just in case I did not find one. That left me finding peace in places where my guard did not have to be up. A place where my brain could stop and rest from studying the game film of life. The staff was always new, and you rarely saw guests enough to say, "Oh yeah, I remember you from the other day." Everyday new stuff to absorb, not enough consistency of anything specific to file as a norm. It was undressing to have no former knowledge to draw from, and the knowledge you were receiving change day to day. All I could do was continue to move forward with my checklist.

Your Minneapolis transitioning was no different than when I found you. You were floating in the middle of the old you and the whatever new you that you end up being. The river bottom was your hotel, where you met the king of transitioning-the way you felt living in that hotel. The uneasiness of constantly being a stranger meeting a stranger would have been your life had you followed his ways.

I do not know what is to come, but that assuredly would have been the death of me.

Anyway, I did not mean to interrupt.

Well thankfully, Saturday my quest for apartments ended. A previous apartment I had looked into had an appointment cancel for a one-bedroom studio. I had only viewed the apartment from the website but was so ready to get out of the hotel, I told them I wanted it sight unseen. "Where do I need to send my deposit?" They still wanted me to view the apartment before depositing anything. I hurriedly dressed, typed the location into my phone and made my way. It turned out to be the perfect location for both my jobs and school. Finally, I had found a place I could start planting seeds of familiarity. That one call changed the pessimistic light that was sneaking passed the hotel room curtains to that light of optimism that sneaks passed the edges of the clouds saying just keep going; I am about to shine on you.

The apartment was perfect and old, that kind of old that felt secure, and solidly settled. It had held off the erosion of its age and the dreadful lived-in smell. Best of all, I could look out my window and see the Mississippi River. I never thought about the Mississippi River being all the way up here, but then again, I never thought I would be at the bottom of one if its tributaries either. Finding a church home in Minneapolis was always "numero uno" on my checklist, but that apartment blessing I had just received had me like, "You better go to church tomorrow!" There were two churches that people back home advised to check out. Since I did not know anything about either, of course, I chose the closest one to the hotel. My GPS led me to the general area of the church, but it had about as hard of time as I did of finding precisely where the church was. I arrived on time, but the temporary search of the actual building caused me to walk in a little late. It was my first time to be in a room with a mass group of people since I had moved. The service was mechanically clinical. It felt like school food, edible but deliberately bland. I was still on a high from what I perceived was blessing from God regarding the apartment, so I was attentive. I wanted to make sure my humanness was not causing a bias toward worship, but it felt like I was on a first date and I was overly anxious. Before I had walked in, I had decided this church would be the one. I decided that because I was tired of looking. Since I had moved, all I had been doing was looking for things- jobs, hotels, stores, apartments and now church. I was exhausted and ready to check off the last thing on my list, but sadly this was not it. I sat there attentively obligatory while devising how I could make this triangle of a church fit my circular needs. By the end of service, I had come to a resolution. I had to visit the other church. I realized sitting on the pew fidgeting I could not settle. I could accept this church, but I could not settle for it. The only way I could accept it was if the other church were worse. I prayed it was not.

I started moving into my apartment the next day. The apartment building was the wise stately gentlemen of the block. There were newer condos on each side of my building, but they lacked the character of time and the gray hair of color faded brick. This was one of those, "If these walls could talk" buildings. As soon as I stepped off the elevator and on to my floor, there was a big glass window that showed more of the Mississippi

River. Watching the river was entrancing, like watching the weather channel- for some reason there was a calming bigness to it all. Knowing that this water is going to travel all the way to Gulf let my brain travel the way I do when I am watching all the different temperatures that the country will experience accompanied by the hypnotic elevator music of the weather channel. My imagination floated as I pondered what I would be doing in each one of those cities. The move did not take too long. I only had one carload, and that consisted mostly of the back seat and trunk. The move was more tedious than strenuous. The multiple trips from the car to the garage elevator, to the building, to building elevator, and finally my apartment was a chore. Once I had everything moved in, I pleasingly looked around at my new space. There's nothing like the feeling of accomplishment, and my accomplishment was more a mental feat than a physical. I had only packed the essential for the move so, minus the inflatable bed, some books, and my laptop, the apartment looked as empty as it did before I moved in. I had told myself before I moved, you are only going to be here for 2 years so pack like it. You don't need a couch, tv, a real bed just the essentials. That talk to myself was good advice, but it was not fully received until I was packing my mid-size car. The limited room of my car stripped my meager packing essentials to the likes of a minimalist. Needless to say, there were a few things that could not make the trip. I went to the store and bought a vacuum cleaner, a tall skinny lamp and two foldable saucer style chairs for the occasional posture switch. Although the apartment lacked those other comfortable amenities of the hotel, the apartment held the advantageous trump card. It was home, and if home is where the heart is, my heart was finally able to let its hair down.

Everything on my checklist had been accomplished except for church, but I checked that off as well, so, now I was in the waiting game- waiting for school to start, job to start, and of course, patiently waiting for next Sunday and another opportunity at finding a church home. I could not remember the last time I was this free with my time. It was truly like being a college student again, going to bed late, reading, drawing, and writing while listening to pod casts and music only to wake around 10am if I wanted to. It was great. I even found a gym that was close by, so I started going there to break up the monotony of my day. With a place to call my own and so well rested, I was ready to investigate all the differences from Tennessee. I observed and soaked Minneapolis like a sponge comparing it all to what I had left back home. I was fully embracing my new environment, but I did hold on to certain habits from home just to feel connected. Aside from only listening to satellite radio, I never watched the local news morning, midday, or night. Instead of watching Minneapolis local news, I would check my phone for the weather. If I wanted to watch the news, I would watch the Nashville local news on my laptop. I was not ready to get to know new weathermen and anchor people. I felt once I did that, I would be totally unplugged from home. It was shocking how much I did not miss tv, nothing invading your space with their thoughts but you. It was total Zen in my apartment- no disturbances but me disturbing me, as I jump from one train to the next train of thought. I was devouring the books I had brought, which in a way was like watching tv. I just was directing and producing the vision myself. My first week had been in my new home had been good. Everything was culminating perfectly. I had been so occupied with getting adjusted that Sunday had snuck up on me quicker than a sinner's Saturday which I did not mind at all. I had anxiously been looking forward to what church number two would be like since church number one last Sunday. I woke up early and left out with a bit of a cushion in case my GPS had similar locating issues as before. Thankfully, there were none. The GPS brought me to the exact location. The parking lot was small but since I arrived so early, I had my choice of the lot. I stayed in the car for a while. I wanted to let some other members walk in before me. That way I could blend in and obscurely worship without being the new guy. After watching a couple of people walk in, I decided to follow in behind a young family, grab a bulletin and scanned the pews looking for the best spot for my plan of incognito. The mid back is always a good seat when trying to blend in. Although I was intently scanning, it was part of my act. I already had in mind exactly where I wanted to sit. It turned out my plan was useless; there weren't enough people to be unseen. I do not think one pew was at capacity, but it felt full. The church felt humid, but instead of moisture, the air was filled with a tangible familial warmth. Smiles say a lot about relations, and it was a lot of genuine smiles in that building. I received and gave out a few myself not to disrupt the feel of the room. The contrast from last Sunday was night and day. I was glad to be there. The service was good and message, solid. If you have been in church your whole life at some point, there really aren't any new bible verses. Everything is repeated and reheated; it is our life experiences that allow it to be absorbed differently each time. I was appreciative of my Sunday worship, and I hoped God was appreciative of my worship efforts to him. I had found my church home! Over the next couple of weeks, my routine went undisturbed. I would wake up around 10, go to the gym, eat lunch, listen to some podcasts, call, or text some people back home, take a nap, read, write, draw, eat dinner and listen to music while taking a shower and get back to reading, writing, drawing until I fell asleep in the wee hours of the night. Every day was the same thing except on Sunday. Sundays were Church day, and it was good to see some familiar faces because during the week, I was still like a kid looking out the window of a road trip wondering when I was going to get there. Sundays and church were my rest stop. I would power up before hitting road again for another week. I was still three weeks away from starting school and my jobs, so meeting people in my everyday setting had not started yet. The members were as comforting as the singing and the sermon. The Sunday before I finally reached my destination of starting school, the Church had some out-of-town visitors. There had only been a handful of visitors since I had been coming, and they were from the neighborhood that the church was in. These visitors were the first I had seen from out of town. The size of this church combined with the small number of churches in Minneapolis made me skeptical of visitors coming to churches anyway. This was not the bible belt of the south I grew up in. In members the church was a "family sized" church although many were not blood related. This was a small transplant led church in a lower income neighborhood, so I was surprised to see visitors outside of the neighborhood. On this Sunday, we had 15 visitors from Houston, Texas. They were visiting for a family reunion being held in the city. I noticed them immediately because they had sat on "my row," in "my seat," and there were so many, they had taken my 2nd option of seating as well. Still no biggie, considering all the other rows were open with plenty of room. I ended up sitting in front of them. Like any minister, but especially a small church minister, you notice big groups. Before he started preaching, he acknowledged the visitors and asked where they were from. They stood up and introduced themselves, explaining the who's,

where's and whys of their visit to Minneapolis.
Because it took so long for them to introduce
themselves, the minister decided to let everybody
else to also stand up for quick meet and greet
before starting the sermon. Typically, on any other
Sunday, there would be maybe 2 or 3 people max
in my vicinity. I would cordially wave to them,
maybe shake hands, and sit back down waiting for
sermon to begin. But this Sunday, I had 15 people
behind me. I expected to cordially turn around, do
my normal routine of shaking a hand, saying hi,
saying glad you are here and then sitting down. As
I turned around, it was an older lady, likely in her
sixties to seventies, but she looked much younger.
I went to shake her hand, but she pulled me in by
my hand and hugged me instead. She hugged me
like she knew me. In that moment, had I not had
my knee on the pew seat, I would have collapsed.
I felt electricity pinging through my connective
tissue. It was as if I was hugging my mom. It was
love in her hug. It was care in her hug. It was my
mom in her hug. I do not know if she saw it in me
or was just a hugger, but I needed it. I do not know
what that "it" was exactly, but I have seen "it"
offered before and thought it was creepy until then.
I was flipping through channels and saw the news
reporting a big LGBTQ equal rights protest. They

were showing the protest from all views and angles. There were thousands of people out there. As they shot back to the reporter onsite, there was a man walking around with a carboard sign behind him that said, "DAD, FREE HUGS." They showed this girl come up to him and they hugged. Two strangers hugged like they knew each other. She hugged him like that was her dad, and she was his daughter. In this moment, I understood that. I understood how you could collapse in a stranger's arms giving you a hug. I had not received a hug since I moved, but I was so busy with completing my checklist that something as common as a hug was not a cause for pause. What is a hug if you do not have a place to stay or a job to maintain? I was moving like everything was normal because it was to me. I did not know that my physiology and psychology had not been disconnecting since I moved. That connection was the same thing that was rekindled when that girl hugged that father. Unbeknownst to her, she had likely been moving about her journey in life in the LGBTQ community ostracized or at least frowned upon from those she likely had always received genuine hugs from. She did not know the importance of that hug, no more than I knew until that lady at church hugged me. The electricity that came from her hugging me was me reconnecting. Touch is the glue which keeps us connected to ourselves. The glue that is necessary for babies to grow and survive. It had been at least a month since I had been hugged. I did not notice it until then, but when it happened, it opened my eyes to how much I had taken touch for granted. It had been such common practice to get and give hugs, I never thought about it. I do not think since I had been born that I had went a week without a hug. Like baby, something in me needed that touch. That hug was like a hard reset to my body and brought all of me back online and running properly. Without human touch, I was becoming a robot in a sense. A robot that had specific tasks to accomplish. That lady at church gave me a quality-of-life validation when she hugged me- a validation I didn't know I needed. When that girl hugged that father giving free hugs, she cried. She cried hard. Those were tears of validation. Any doubts of skepticism I may have had when I read that article about the importance of touch disappeared after my hugging experience with that lady, but not just for babies. It is for everybody.

I agree. That makes good sense. When you first started, I was a little worried. I did not know where your story was going.

By the way, I started getting my feeling back about halfway through me talking, but since I couldn't make out what I was feeling, I kept talking, while trying to figure out what was going on at the same time.

Mirrors vs Windows

Did you figure it out what you were feeling because you had a lot to say? All of it necessary, just unexpected compared to your other answers.

No, I did not figure it out. I mean, I know I am in the water but I feel something clinging to me, and there is a pressure on my head that I cannot make out. It reminds me of a helmet, but that does not make sense. It is weird, but so is this whole situation. I would ask you, but I know how that will play out. At this point, I will just trust your guidance. I am sure I will find out everything soon enough.

That is very mature. Where is all this confidence in me coming from?

It's more so the fact that I am making progress than it is maturity. Getting some of my senses back has made it much easier to accept my situation.

What do you mean by accept your situation? This is not an acceptable situation for you.

Exactly, but I had to accept I was here first. I accepted the bottom of the river as my starting point and not a landing point. I was fighting where I landed, but you cannot fight where you land. You can ease the fall which is what I think you were trying to do. You showed up mid fall, and I fought against you. So, you let gravity have me. I thought I was stuck until you reappeared. I figured if you were still here then I must not be stuck. Why else would a guide stay around if they could not guide anymore? I just needed to listen and let you lead me to my senses. My senses would compass me out of here.

Yep, all you had to do was just answer a couple of questions.

You are right, but I do not really understand what you were asking at first. Likely my fault, but regardless of all that, let's keep moving. Also, do not think I have forgotten about my questions for you either. The sooner I finish your questions, the sooner I can get to mine.

Or the sooner you finish your questions the sooner you could find your way out of here.

I want both. What is the next question?

You should be able to see what is next. It is Sight.
Why can you see?

My sight has been on decline since I was born. I
was around twelve when my optometrist jokingly
said, your eyes are pretty much useless to you. My
eyes have been operating on their last breath ever
since. Not that it matters much in my current state,
but I am legally blind. Without contacts or glasses
I am in trouble, so although not being able to see at
all is much worse, it has not been as traumatic as
the loss of my other senses. I cannot remember the
last time I did not wake up in a water-colored
painting as my hands blindly searched for my
glasses, everything a smear of blurred and blended
colors camouflaging together to hide my glasses.
There were times I would be looking directly at
my glasses and dismiss them as something else as I
continued searching. When I finally circled back to
that overlooked spot, I would have to laugh at
myself for seeing so poorly that I could not notice
my glasses staring there, directly at me. It was easy
to forget about not being able to see at night.
Twenty-twenty dreams with high-definition clarity
were no problem as I slept. Only when I woke was

I quickly reminded of my inferior vision. The frantic search for my glasses each morning or the rush to put my contacts in was from the shock of vulnerability of looking around and not being able to make out anything I was looking at.

If your eyesight is that bad, you could not see anything in this water, not that I advise you opening your eyes in this water anyway.

True, I am sure it is murky down here, but regardless when I get my sight, you better believe I am going to look. It cannot be any worse than waking up in the morning.

Yea, you are right, so why do you see?

You know this could have two answers.

Huh? Explain.

Up until now, all the answers have fallen under the umbrella of politeness. So, to say I see for others only makes sense based on the previous, but what is wrong with me using my eyes for me? If the reason I am in the mirror is to improve me, hence helping others, it is the window vs the mirror. I can look through the window for someone else or look to the mirror for me. In my eyes, in my eyes there should not be an either-or?

You probably should not start with in your eyes considering your current and past condition of eyesight. All I asked was why do you see? I did not give you an either-or to deliberate with. You did that. Yes, both serve a purpose, but one is short sighted purpose. The surface of this river has a natural reflection. You could stare at your reflection all day, like you would a mirror, but how does looking at yourself improve yourself? You are only seeing a surface level reflection of your surface level self. Even a window holds a reflection, but it's only when you look past yourself that you can see. "Perfecting" yourself or making yourself better as you say, only deals with how you view yourself. Your true reflection is shown in how you show yourself to others, not a mirror. A mirror is short sighted because it only considers how you see yourself. As you said already, your vision is bad. How does your bad vision improve you? The only way to improve you is to look past your river-like reflection into the depths of your vision. How you see for others reflects you. A mirror only shows you what it wants you to see. Your mirrored

*reflection is a moot point of view that cataracts the
purpose of sight.*

I remember my dad would always tell me do not
date girls that are always in the mirror.

Exactly. Your dad knew.

He knew, but all the girls I liked were in the
mirror. So, I had to learn the hard way, when I
could have just listened.

So, you were blind but now you see, huh?

Ha, Jokes?

*Well, you should have just listened. Everything
does not have to make sense instantaneously;
wisdom is instruction for tomorrow. Common
sense is for today.*

Well, common sense says Windows over Mirror. I
never should have seen it any other way. I
remember my junior year of college my cousin and
I lived in some off-campus apartments. It was
super late to be up, even for a college kid. I had the
front bedroom that looked out into our pavilion.

My window sat up high above the ground, so I always kept the window open to hear who was coming and going into our courtyard. We stayed in building C, which from a helicopter view was shaped like a U. If you had a front bedroom in any apartment in our building, you could see everything coming and going. It was about 2am when I heard a car pull up and park which was strange because we mostly had medical students and single parent families. there were only a handful of undergrad students like me in our building. We typically were the only neighbors coming in after twelve am. There was nothing going on in the city so none of us were out that I knew of. I looked out hoping to catch our next-door neighbor bringing over some late company so I could yell out the window, "Now you know better that that." Instead, I see my neighbor who lived directly on the other side of our pavilion. I rarely saw her much, as she was a med student. Med students were more aberrations than neighbors. I assume because they were always studying. Just as I was about to turn my blinds closed, I see a man come from behind this wall that fences our pavilion. He is creeping toward her in a crawl like stance. She is steadily walking to the door and does not suspect a thing. My heart started to race as my brain went supercomputer, going through every computation and outcome to best solve this situation safely. I hopped up and ran to my front door, which leads to the main door to get into my part of the building. I crouched down and opened my building door that leads outside to insinuate someone was coming out, and then I slammed the door as hard as I could. I look up to see the man running off and woman looking toward my door. She did not even know what potentially was about to happen to her. I always thought we would cross paths one day, and I would tell her what happened, but that day never came. And I was ok with that; I did not do it for credit. I did it because I saw it. I saw it, and I reacted. I was on such an adrenaline rush after that, I do not know if went to sleep. My cousin was out of town so I had nobody tell. The way I felt, to have potentially saved someone's life was sublime. If they had that feeling in a pill, I would take one every day. I felt complete.

You do not need the pill, you just do it again.

What do you mean?

Open your eyes and you will see.

Whoa, are you? But how?

Yes, I am and that pill you are looking for, that feeling you talk about is how. That is exactly why I am here. I am here because I know that sublimeness. That is your purpose being fed. You do not need a pill to be purposeful. You just need your common senses-hear, taste, smell, feel, and see. That fulfillment you described, you can have that every day if you use your senses.

So, Wait you're here for me? But you are...no, no this is not possible.

It is possible.

How? Why are you here, talking to me?

I guess it is your turn to ask the questions. Since you can move now, let us talk and move. How, you asked? How did I go from picking up some food for my family, to suddenly everything I knew being taken from me? My wife, kids, family, friends, anything I was familiar with was gone. In flash, I was being transported to a whole new world. The transition was so new and loud. The noises, lights,

speed, all of it was so different my brain could not
multitask quick enough for comprehension of it all.
This stimulation overload caused me to blackout
as my brain needed to quiet me down so it could
function. I woke up to a clinical simulation of my
natural environment. Everything was correct.
Nothing was out of place. It had a calculated feng
shui. Not made for the living, but for the looking. It
was fraudulent.

It was like you were living in a forged Picasso
trying to pass for the original, but it wore no flaws.

Picasso?

He is a famous painter. His paintings are worth a
lot of money. There have been forgers who have
tried to recreate his paintings for money. The lack
of flaws from the original is how they usually get
caught.

Yes, that was the giveaway. This place had
confused perfection with correction. Perfection
can only be seen in flaws. To make something
beautiful and absent of all the disruption around it
is perfection. We were all made perfect in the flaws
of our natural surroundings. Our instincts are

developed in these pitfalls of life, but what do you do when everything has been corrected for the purpose of perfection? All my instincts that naturally meshed in my environment did not fit into this cosmetic world. Although thankful to be alive, I did not feel I was living, more so, being kept alive. I could not even survive in my new world; any option of purpose had been corrected away. I was in a safe proof room with no door to my old life. I do not know how many days I spent in the same place thinking about my family. Nothing in this artificial world expressed reality. Nothing aged, nothing moved or changed colors. Every day was the same day. Everyday Looked the same. Everyday smelled the same. I was the only thing that could change or move. Little did I know with each waking day I was acclimating to my stagnated new life. Until one day I stopped moving. I stopped changing.

You finally had been corrected. You had been there so long you became a fixture on the canvas of the master forger of your new life.

I do not know how long I was there. I know I stayed in the same place, the same way. I assume I was there long enough for this so-called forger to grow tired of me. Since I was not moving, he moved me. Just as quick as I was yanked from my family, I was taken from the canvas of his painting. I did not blackout this time as most of my senses had been dampened due to my lethargy. I remember being thrown into loud, gushing, and powerfully moving water. I had never experienced a current like the one I was thrown into. I fought to get out of the gravity of the current. Eventually I managed to get to quieter water, only to realize this environment was not for me either. It had the familiar flaws of reality but was missing the sustainability I needed. This water was not for me. It was missing something. The way my body was reacting I knew this was not living water, and I did not have long. I was fighting so hard to get out of that current, I had no time to notice my surroundings. Surviving was all I had on my brain. Being couped up in the safety of an artificial world, I had forgotten what it was like to try to survive. The sudden exertion of energy I used struggling to get out of that powerful current awoke all my senses. As things settled, I still could not fully catch my breath alerting me I was in foreign waters. I floated, looking around and wondering about my family? I was finally free. I should have been excited. I was free to move around, but around where and why? This place was not for me. Death was always present since the moment I was born, but here, death was an incessant tap on my shoulder. I was chasing oxygen, and these shallow breaths I was taking did not allow a second of forgetfulness that death was near. I never thought about death back home. I think because I envisioned that death would have had to come find me. Find me living, but here what could I do but die? Die waiting for death, just watching my time tick away. I wanted death to come get me. I wanted death to find me living, and possibly be so intrigued with what he finds me doing he waits. Instead, I was waiting. Waiting and floating. Floating and waiting. I was one with the current, lazily meandering my way to meet death. I was going with the flow of my circumstances. Anxious, but resolved, I closed my eyes and tried to control my breathing. My morbid Lamaze was broken by a boulder splashing down on me. It fell with such force, that I had no time to avoid it. Instinctively, I moved just enough to not get smashed but accidently ended up clinging on to it as it carried me down. That boulder ended up being you. I had grab you by your head. My senses, already on high alert from trying to dodge you, were so sensitive that my body read you, and I

picked up your senses. I immediately felt our
bodies were sharing a familiarity, and instinctively
my body reacted with empathy. As the force of the
fall was still carrying us down, I found a harmony
between us. We were singing the same notes. Notes
of displacement in an environment not meant for
us. You were unconscious, not breathing, so I
breathed for both us. The way I caught you, I held
on to you covering your eyes nose mouth and ears,
until we had stopped sinking. Floating between the
surface and the bottom of the river, I found
balance in my personal limbo. You were my
tangible eureka moment that interrupted my
thoughts of how I envisioned death possibly
finding me. You brought an opportunity of purpose
to these vain waters, that even my current
condition, I could possibly die a life worth living.
Possibly a life worth death's grace, but only if I
did not wait for it. You made me stop and think,
what is the point of spending the rest of my
remaining life waiting to get something that I will
not live long enough to keep? Once you die, what
is death? You cannot do anything with it. You are
dead, so why wait on that? Death is for the living,
so why not try to live? Floating in the middle of
this river, I decided I would try to live, so I forced
myself to breath deep. When I did, I was able to

breathe for you and me. In that instance, I realized no matter where I am in life, I can give. And when I give is when I live. I was lazily floating toward death, but when I gave you air, everything flipped. You brought meaning to the phrase "It is better to give than to receive." I never thought about wanting to receive death, in correlation with that phrase. I never said it is better to give my life than to receive death, but you changed my paradigm of life in this environment. It was not about what this place could give me, but what I could give it. I had resigned to going with the flow and waiting for my get my death stamp, but instead I got you. Seeing you in the water not breathing showed me an opportunity to give. While we were attached, I sensed that you were okay with dying, but not at peace with it. In fact, it was the lack of your peace that okayed the dying. As you came to and we talked, I could hear how deep you were into your feelings. You had dug so deep into your emptiness that it had devalued your life. I asked all those why questions of your senses to show you what you brought out of me when you fell on me out of your turmoil and into peace.

You could not find peace because your equilibrium was off. The economy of our souls plays in the balance of supply and demand. You had the supplies needed for peace, but your demands were only for yourself. There was nothing you could get that would satisfy your demands and fill your void. If you never got out of your demands, your supplies would be like closeout items on a clearance aisle. Although for different reasons, I knew this to be true because I had just put my supplies on the shelves. I thought in an environment not meant for me, what could I supply? Whose demand could I meet, but when I breathed for you, I got my answer. When I supplied sight, smell, hearing, touch, and taste for you it brought equilibrium to this limbo. However, the weight of your demands, that heaviness is what anchored you to the riverbed. I stayed connected, floating above. Still breathing for you, I left you there in the abyss of your demands, hoping you would find your way before it was too late for the both of us. I felt physically there was nothing else I could say or do. You were too indignant to listen and too heavy to hold. Until you answered the whys of your existent, you would never understand that your supply was the key to a peaceful inner economy.

Why did you stay connected to me? You could have died. Do not get me wrong, I am thankful you stayed, but why risk it.

No, there is no 'could have' died. We will die, but like I said, death is going to have to come find me living. I did not know how to live until I breathed for you. Breathing for you, took my mind off my last breath. I am sure if we never had met, we would both be dead by now. So, there was no risk of dying, it was only a risk of living.

Did you know Fin would be down there?

No. I was quite surprised to see him down there? I never would have suspected he could make it down here?

So you knew Fin pretty well?

Not so much him, but I know of his type pretty well.

His type?

His character, his motive of operation.

And what did you think of him?

I did not think anything of him at first, just listened
to him talk. He made well known from the
beginning he was heavy on life, which I thought in
your case would not be bad for you to hear.
Anything that could potentially cause you to stop
sinking and look upward could not hurt. Did I
agree with how he was moving? Not at all. Open
ended lifestyle, running from the closures of life is
a fairytale. At some point, there are no more new
stories or experiences that you have not already
dabbled in and naturally the only interest left is
how it all ends. If it has not already, his childish
approach toward life will eventually lead to
reruns. That is why he was so eager for you to tag
along; you were something new. Only in our youth
do we enjoy starting things and not finishing them.
The gift of youthful exploration, being able to
move from one thing to the next, without a thought
of finishing any of it, is the curse of avoidance
when practice by the mature. Fin is always on the
go, thinking he could avoid his pain. Only children
believe they can live pain free. Experience tells
you that life has a storage bin of pain with your
name on it and its nothing you can do about it, but
maturity is the reward for those that face it. Hence
the phrase growing pains. You cannot run from
life's discomforts and find peace. Fin would rather

settle for the pleasures of new beginning and no endings. Anything to temporarily take his mind off what is chasing him. Thankfully, his conversation caused you to look up from your feelings. Although, he almost convinced you of his lifestyle.

No, I was not going with him.

I do not know. From what I heard he was about to close the deal.

What would you have done?

You mean what would we have done? We would have died. If I had let you go, you would have drowned. You would have been Fin's new story to tell his next new stranger. As for me, like I said before I would have died eventually.

You would have let me go?

Even if I wanted to, I could not have kept up with him while breathing for us, but Fin knew that. He knew you could not keep up with him. Fin is opportunistic solo artist, and you would have been a circumstantial backup singer. As soon as his tune changed, he would have left you dead with no remorse.

It's unbelievably wild how casual you are with death. You're so matter of fact when you say, "We would've died."

Us specifically trying to keep up with Fin, death would have smelled blood in the water, so, yes, we would have died. But death is going to come whether you want it or not, but life is given to you. Therefore, your life was intentional, death is just a by-product. You were intended to be here, there is nothing casual about that. I gave you air because I intended for you to live. Me giving you the ability to breathe snoozed deaths alarm. In this unsustainable situation I could still give, and nothing is better for you than to give. if I can give, I am in the best place I can be. There is an internal reward from giving that keeps my mind off death, until death comes to get me.

This place, not meant for you is the best place for you?

Yes, you only have two options in life. Everything revolves around giving or receiving. We know giving is better than receiving, so If I am in a place

I can give, I'm in a place meant for me.

Yea, that reminds me of a conversation I had at the barbershop about working at McDonald's.

McDonalds? Is this same place your sister worked?
Yes, but a different store.

McDonalds must be a popular place.

It is well known, but in regard to working there, let's just say it could be seen as less than ideal situation. My sister only lasted a couple of months.

What do you mean?

A situation not meant for your survival. Let me explain. There was a grandfather in the chair holding court about his grandson needing to get a job. He said McDonalds was hiring, and he knew the manager. All his grandson had to do was fill out the application, and he would have the job. He was upset that his grandson did not want to get a job at a fast-food place like McDonalds. He said they do not pay enough, and he would find his own job. The entire time his grandson was sitting there quiet, respectfully listening, but I could see he was getting upset. As more ears started to lean in on the conversation, his leg started shaking. He was ready to explode when one of the other barbers said, I can feel where grandson is coming from. I worked at McDonalds around his age.

When I first started working there, I hated it. During the interview, the manager sold the heck out of being a McDonalds employee really highlighting all the perks. To a constantly hungry teenager the food perks were music to my ears. The food privilege sounded great, but after my first paycheck I realized free food is not free, When you are not free, the check looked like burger cropping slavery. You could work as many hours as you wanted, overtime with time and half, whatever. It still was not enough money to live on. McDonalds was not that kind of place. Luckily, I was still living under my parents' roof, and me working was more of a next step in responsibility, than it was in financial necessity. But had I been dependent on this money I would have rather stayed home and been broke because these paychecks never compensated for the value of time loss, and that ate me up on the inside. Every day, I clocked in, I could not shake the thought of what I was getting paid. I could not understand how anyone that was not in a similar situation to me would choose to work here, until I met Martha. Martha was an older lady I worked with. When I met her, she had been with McDonalds for seven years. She showed me the way. She changed my whole outlook. Martha did not share my sentiments toward McDonalds at all. There was not a time we worked together that she was not genuinely having a ball. The customers loved her; the regulars asked about her when they did not see her. The unpleasant/jerk customers did not faze her. She wore an armor of "Bobby McFerrin" that was impenetrable from the verbal and nonverbal cues of rude customer conversation. Even when the managers were acting tyrannical, she kept it moving without missing a beat. Not me, this job was not paying me enough to take anything but the best behavior from all involved. I felt stuck and my mood reflected that, but Martha moved with an oblivion of ownership. I could not understand it. One day, feeling I was nearing my wits end, disgruntled I asked her, "How do you do it?" You seem to always be flying above the storm. She asked when I was taking my lunch and we could talk then. I did not think my question warranted her sharing my limited lunch time, but I was curious. We sat down near the back of the store

close to the restrooms. She told me I was not the
first person to ask her how she could be so happy
while working here. She said the problem is
familiarity. You think McDonalds is here to serve
you like it always has. I bet you grew up on the
happy meals and soft serve ice cream cones. You
have been programmed since you were little that
McDonalds is supposed to make you happy, but
instead of a burger and a toy you want a
McDonalds paycheck to do that. The difference is
you are McDonalds now, it is not about you
anymore, it is about them. Why do I enjoy it here?
How can I genuinely smile? Because I can make
them happy. The customer. You are so worried
about getting paid you ignore your ability. We
have the ability to give, and not just give what they
paid for but what they do not deserve, you. You
can give them what they paid for, and let that be
that. That is a job, or you can give them you. That
is joy. I try to give me every day to everybody. If
you are in place where you can give yourself, you
are where you need to be! I do not work anywhere
for the money; you will die inside out. What is
money if there is no joy in how you got it. Work
for the give, and You will live inside out. You
know how I know this is true? The hook up.
People come in here order a burger but cannot

afford the fries. I hook them up. You see them contemplating, maybe counting their money, asking how much the tax is. There are always ways to give people what they need if you are looking to give. (you) When you clock back in, your first customer no matter what they order, I want you to look for the give. Give them more than what they paid for. Hook them up, even if they could have paid for it. The hook up says I see you and you matter. That is what giving you means. Giving someone what they do not deserve. That is the real special sauce, it is not that mac stuff. Giving *you* is the secret ingredient to life. Tell me how you feel after you give *you.* You will understand why you see me bouncing around laughing and smiling once you get a hit of what undeserved giving feels like. When you see the power of giving, you will recognize the power in you. That will change how you see this place.

The barber said that changed his life. He told the grandson you do not work at McDonalds for the money. You work at McDonalds to hook people up. That is where you will find the joy that pays you more than money. He said he worked at McDonalds until he graduated high school and left for barber college. His advice to that grandson is the same wavelength you have been on since we met. You hooked me up!

I hooked you up so you could see you are here to hook people up, too. That was the only way to get you back to the surface.

And it did, your hook up, hooked me up to why I am here. Sorry for everything earlier and thank you for everything you have done. You gave me another chance.

Accepted and thank you for the opportunity to give. You ready?

Yes, I am ready.

You ready to give?

Without a doubt.

Okay, on the count of three, I want you take a deep breath and open your eyes. One, two, three.

Man! The sky has never looked so good as when you think you will never see it again.

Very true.

I can breathe on my own! I can smell this awful water. I will pass on tasting this water. I would rather my first taste be something more pleasant.

Like McDonald's?

Ha, there you go with the jokes. Who knows, but it definitely will not be this water.

Hey this is my home you are talking about.

Well, you said it was unsustainable. I am just reiterating that a little bit.

I understand, jokes. Well congratulations! You made it!

No, we made it! Without you there would be no me.

Ok we made it, but it is time for us to go our separate ways.

I wish there were away for you to go with me. I feel like I owe you a way out. Plus, you turned out not to be so bad.

Oh really? That is funny. You turned out not to be so bad.

You sure I could not interest you in your previous abode. It was the perfect feng shui environment with all the views.

I am positive! I am right where I am supposed to be. Now it is time for you to be.
But where will you go? How will you live?

I do not know but I am not worried about that. I just know I will be giving until I am not living. Maybe I will run into Fin, and as you said, see if he will let me hook him up. Just know I will not be waiting for death.

Oh yeah, one more thing. Now that I can clearly see, what is your name? I would like to put a name to your face.

My name is O'Shean. Now go!
Hey no splashing! That almost got in my mouth!

Wait- What?

Hey! The dead has arisen.

What? Where am I?

Boy, you were knocked out when got here. I nudged you, shook the chair, even turned up the music in the shop. Nothing I did woke you up. You were breathing so I figured you had a long night. Here, let me get you a mirror. I assumed you wanted your regular edge up and taper. How does it look?

Wait, wait, wait! I have been sleeping this whole time?

Yeah man you were in comatose, talking in your sleep and everything. You must have been tired.

I don't know. This is wild, I thought I had already left the barbershop.

*Nah man, you are here, in my chair, and in case
you are wondering you have not already paid yet.
Now come on, how your haircut look?*

My fault Sheem. Yeah, everything looks good.

*Cool. Let me hit you one more time with the
alcohol spray before you get out of here.*
Ok.

There you go. You good.

Appreciate that Sheem. Keep the change. My bad
about falling asleep. I have never done that in my
life.

*It's all good. I know you got a lot on your mind
right now. Prayers up bro, for you and the fam.*

Yes sir. Thanks.

*Oh. Yo, Trey. I forgot here is your paper. It fell on
the floor while you were sleeping.*

Paper?

Your newspaper. Knoxville News.

Oh yea. I forgot all about that. I fell asleep reading it while I was waiting for you.

Why do you have Knoxville paper anyway?

Ask Vee about Ten Speed. He came in this morning and Vee got to messing with him, which led to me and this paper. You know how it goes around here. Ask Vee for the full rundown.

Yeah, I know. Take it easy bro.

Will do. I will take that paper back up to Vee on the way out.

What up Trey? Sheem got you right back there?

Yeah man. He did his thing. Here go Ten Speed paper, too. I do not know if he is coming back or not.

I am sure he is coming back. Like clockwork right before quitting time.

Sheem asked about why I had a Knoxville paper. I told him you would fill him in.

Yeah, I got him, but fill my guy in over there about why you work at places like McDonalds. You remember that story.

Yeah, I remember it like I just told it. Vee I got a lot going on today. I cannot be in this barbershop all day.

You right. You right. well, you're a teacher; give him the cliff notes version.

Cliff notes version?

Yea short and sweet.

Alright, real quick.

Wait, hold up. Who is that?

Barbershop patrons: who is that?

Man, ya'll tripping.

Aw man. That is your auntie! Let her come in this time.

Hey, Vee I will holla at you.

Here she come.

Auntie! What are you doing?

I was about to walk in to see if you were still in there.

I told you I was going to walk back.

It is too cold, and this main road is too busy to be walking with no sidewalks.

Alright, just get in the car.

Why you rushing me? You are acting like your uncle.
Because you do not need to be going into the barbershop. You not going to have Unc mad at me.

Mad at you? I am grown.
I hear you, but you need to listen to me. Next time just call or text. I will let Unc explain to you why later.

Your uncle does not need to tell me nothing. The barbershop is not the only place a woman can get hit on.

Well, I do not want to hear or see it where I get my haircut. Why are you not home anyway? Have you been waiting this whole time?

Heaven's no! Yo uncle got to the house late and all the pancakes were gone. He got to pouting, so I was running back out the grocery store to get some more buttermilk. I thought about you, so I stopped to see if you were ready yet.

I appreciated that, very kind, loving, thoughtful…

But…

…but I told you I was going to walk.

I know, but aren't you happy I came back by? It is too cold.

I see you going to do what you want to do regardless.

Now you get it. Now how do I get back to the grocery store from here?

Turn left. Is there any more food besides the pancakes?

No, everything gone.

You see that McDonalds up on the right? The grocery store is next to it. Drop me off at the McDonalds and I will walk over.

But I was going to have you run in and get the buttermilk real quick, so I do not have to park.

For real? I hope that is not why you came by to pick me up?

Nephew do not be like that. Just run in real quick for me please. I will pay for your McDonalds.

Well now that you have passed it, I guess so.

Thank you. Here is my card. It is in the milk section.

Really, who would of thought?

Just a little a jokey joke.

Whatever.

Whoa, did you steal it?

What?

That was fast! You were in and out.

Here is your card and your receipt Auntie. You
will say anything.

*With a smile on my face! Now next stop the Golden
Arches.*

You do not have to pay for it either.

No, its fine.

Ok

Here- take my card again.

Drive thru looks slow. Park, and I will go inside.

10 minutes pass……

Nephew?

Auntie, why are you calling?
It has been twenty minutes. What are you doing in there?

It has been more like ten. They are making everything fresh. Plus, I got breakfast food and lunch food.

Breakfast and lunch? Hurry up! You know your uncle hungry.

Thank you for waiting for me Auntie.

Dang boy did you order for a family? Why do you have so many bags?

I don't know.

Huh, what do you mean you do not know? Where is my card and my receipt?

Here is your card. I do not know where the receipt is. It is probably in one of the bags.

*Well, you need to find it because let me find out
you spent over ten dollars for some simple
McDonalds! Look like you ordered the whole
menu.*
You know that bridge up ahead that leads into my
Dad's neighborhood? When we get to it, let me
out. I will walk home from there.

Did you hear what I said?

I heard you Auntie.

Well?
Well, I will make sure I get the receipt to you.

*I did not mean to bring in the uncomfortable
silence; I just cannot believe you got all that food.*

It is all good Auntie. Silence is not bad. That is
why I wanted to walk. Help sort some thoughts
out. Also, I did not use your card for the food. I
know better than that. Here is the receipt though.
You can let me out right up here. I can see the
bridge.

Nephew. I was tripping, wasn't I?

It is all good and it is all love. Thank you for coming back to check on me. Oh yeah, here is your money from the barbershop. I will see you back home.

Hey! O'Shean! Can you hear me down there? I don't know what happened this morning, but what I dreamed felt more real than anything I have ever experienced. If a dream can mimic reality that well, some of it must be real. So, if by chance you are part of that realness, I never got to tell you thank you. Thank you for showing me the way, and I got you something for you too. I could not just talk about McDonalds and not hook you up with any. I didn't have a clue what you would like so I got you some of my favorites. Thanks for everything again. You gave me life, and I will never forget that! Hope you enjoy it.

An Article in Ten Speed's newspaper from Knoxville: **Who are O'Shean and Finnick? Read article to find out.**

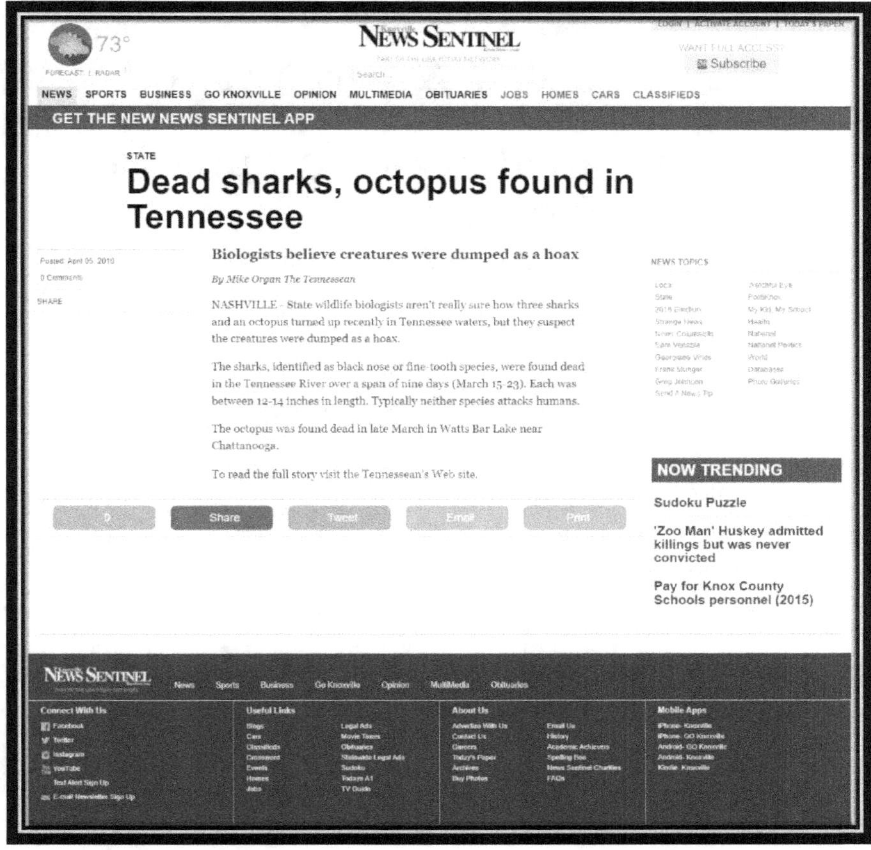

STATE

Dead sharks, octopus found in Tennessee

Biologists believe creatures were dumped as a hoax

Posted: April 05, 2010
0 Comments

SHARE

By Mike Organ The Tennessean

Search...

NEWS SENTINEL
PART OF THE USA TODAY NETWORK

73°

By Mike Organ The Tennessean
Posted: **April 05, 2010**   0

NASHVILLE - State wildlife biologists aren't really sure how three sharks and an octopus turned up recently in Tennessee waters, but they suspect the creatures were dumped as a hoax.

The sharks, identified as black nose or fine-tooth species, were found dead in the Tennessee River over a span of nine days (March 15-23). Each was between 12-14 inches in length. Typically neither species attacks humans.

The octopus was found dead in late March in Watts Bar Lake near Chattanooga.

To read the full story visit the Tennessean's Web site.

Works Mentioned in the Book

Zemeckis, Robert. *Forrest Gump*. Paramount Pictures, 1994.

Tolkien, J. R. R. *The Lord of the Rings*. HarperCollins, 1991.

"X Games." *Wikipedia*, Wikimedia Foundation, 28 Feb. 2021, en.wikipedia.org/wiki/X_Games

"Lassie." *Wikipedia*, Wikimedia Foundation, 16 Mar. 2021, en.wikipedia.org/wiki/Lassie_(1954_TV_series)

Howard, Ron. *A Beautiful Mind*. Universal Pictures, 2001.

Craven, Wes, and Robert Shaye. *A Nightmare on Elm Street*. New Line Cinema, 1984.

"McDonald's." *Wikipedia*, Wikimedia Foundation, 24 Feb. 2021, en.wikipedia.org/wiki/McDonald%27s.

Organ, M. (2010). 'Dead Sharks, Octopus Found
in Tennessee River'. Knoxville News
Sentinel, 5 April Available at:
https://archive.knoxnews.com/news/state/dea
d-sharks-octopus-found-in-tennessee-ep-
408735594-358815831.html/ (Accessed: 17
March 2021)

Autobiography

80's Baby…born year

Preschool…Graduated

Elementary School…Graduated

Middle School…Graduated

High School…Graduated

Junior College…Graduated

University…Graduated

Post College…Graduated

Started a business…www.aulookgood.com

Wrote a book.

There was a lot of life stuff that happened between these milestones that made me who I am like LIFE, DEATH, & McDonalds, and the same goes for you.